W9-AAV-445

Marc

※ March 25-2016
April 24, 2016 — I read

This book came to me a few days before your STAR performance @ the "FOX", such sweet passing out + the voage to return.... the aliveness of the moment.

to marc now, my sweet, sweet, husband

THE HOLY MAN

ALSO BY SUSAN TROTT

THE
HOLY
MAN

SUSAN
TROTT

RIVERHEAD BOOKS
New York
1995

RIVERHEAD BOOKS
a division of G. P. Putnam's Sons
Publishers Since 1838
200 Madison Avenue
New York, NY 10016

Copyright © 1995 by Susan Trott
All rights reserved. This book, or parts thereof,
may not be reproduced in any form without permission.
Published simultaneously in Canada

Library of Congress Cataloging-in-Publication Data

Trott, Susan.
      The holy man / by Susan Trott.
            p.   cm.
      I.   Title.
PS3570 . R594H58   1995   94-37573 CIP
813'. 54—dc20
ISBN I-57322-002-7

Book design by Marysarah Quinn

Printed in the United States of America
10   9   8   7   6   5   4   3   2   I

This book is printed on acid-free paper. ∞

TO ROY

CONTENTS

THE HOLY MAN

1
THE LINE

There was a holy man who lived in a hermitage on a mountain. Although solitary, it was not strictly a hermitage because some monks lived there with him. Even before the world began to seek him out, he was rarely alone.

When word got out about him, people came to see him during the summer months when the hermitage was accessible, first a few people, then more and more until there was a long line climbing the steep mountain path single file—tens, hundreds, and then thousands, some of whom never made it to his door before the snows came and forced their return.

There were no inns so the pilgrims had to be prepared to camp, which wasn't a hardship as the weather was warm and dry. The views were outstanding and wildflowers flanked the path. At night, the stars were dazzling. However it did take strength to carry the camping gear and food, so anyone who was frail did not attempt to see the holy man who, in any case, was not a healer.

The line moved slowly, but it moved continuously during the few hours a day he welcomed people. In fact, those who were near the head of the line and could observe were amazed by how many people he managed to see, even though they were admitted one at a time.

Sometimes the pilgrims had to step aside for one of the monks who lived with the holy man as he or she stepped rapidly and lightly up the path, carrying supplies from the town ten miles below. These men and women were easily distinguished by their wheat-colored robes.

Those in the line never saw the departing pilgrims who went out the back door and down another path to the bottom of the mountain because the upward path, which was called the Hermitage Trail, was too narrow to take two-way traffic.

2

THE
HERMITAGE

The hermitage was a two-story, whitewashed wooden building built on a rock foundation. It was plain, rugged, and square with a peaked roof. There was no ornament—no cross on the roof, Star of David over the door, no stone Buddha in the garden. No garden for that matter. It was a no-frills hermitage.

It faced east and was a few hundred yards from the actual mountain peak. Above treeline, there were marvelous boulders strewn about, shaped by time and cataclysm, finished by rain, snow, and wind.

At the base of one boulder was a small pond, the

source of which was an underground spring, which provided pure water for the hermitage. There were many such springs on the mountain, some of which formed falls and streams that joined with rainwater and snowmelt to flow to the reservoir in the town.

Flamboyant birds and flowers adorned the gray rocks, and the sky was an unstained canvas for clouds and flyways.

When the door was opened wide, the next pilgrim in line, waiting beyond the gate, would be summoned forth by a man in a wheat-colored robe, a small, nondescript-looking person.

"Yes?" he would ask when the pilgrim reached the threshold.

"I have come to see the holy man."

"Follow me, please."

He or she would follow the small man through the house, along a hallway with doorways open to various rooms into which the pilgrim would peek hastily, but the monk ahead was moving so very quickly through the house that the pilgrim couldn't linger but literally had to rush after him.

In no time at all they had passed through the entire

first floor of the house and were at a large door similar to the one the pilgrim had entered. It was the back door. The monk opened it wide and said, "Goodbye."

"But I have come to see the holy man!" said the visitor plaintively.

"You have seen me," he gently replied.

And the next thing the pilgrim knew he would be outside, the door solidly closed behind him.

This is why the line moved so rapidly and how the holy man got to see so many people—or so many people got to see him. The trip through the house was twenty seconds, add another twenty for greetings and partings, another twenty for returning to the front door, and what you have is a person a minute.

Most times the holy man would add, "If you look on everyone you meet as a holy person, you will be happy," which added seven seconds.

Rushing back and forth through the house in this way was a lot of footwork for the holy man, who was seventy-two years old, so periodically he took five-minute rests.

Rarely, but sometimes, which were happy times for him, he sat down and talked to a pilgrim.

3

FEELINGS

What did the pilgrims feel about being given such short shrift after their long inchworm trudge up the mountain?

Most of them, like most people everywhere, were nice. Maybe, per capita, there were more nice people in the line than elsewhere because of the nature of the destination—good people wanting to be better people.

Still, even the nicest among them, when the door shut on their departure, felt some of these feelings:

wronged, hurt, cheated, disappointed, betrayed, ill-used, angry.

But it was amazing how fleeting this letdown was because, as they stood outside the door, somewhat dazed, feeling any or all of the above, they began to review their visit to the holy man and to understand.

The door had been opened to them.

How many places would this happen in a world of peepholes, locks, bolts, and bars?

The door had been opened wide and the one-man reception committee had stood there, eyes alight, a small smile, saying, "Yes?"—a "how may I help you?" sort of yes.

Whereas the pilgrim had not greeted him at all, had not introduced himself, said hello, how are you, may I please come in, but, instead, full of his own importance, his own mission, had treated the door-opener as the lowliest servant, saying, "I've come to see the holy man."

And the door-opener, realizing the visitor's mission had already been accomplished, showed him out.

Thinking this, the pilgrim felt very sorry about his behavior and vowed that he would come again next summer and do differently.

He tried to remember what the holy man looked like and couldn't, because he hadn't looked at him. He wouldn't recognize him if the same man opened the door next year. But no matter. He would be courteous and respectful to whosoever opened the door. In fact, he would be gracious to everyone from now on, imagining that everyone was the holy man, that everyone indeed had holiness in him. This would be very hard. Still he would try. Because that was what he had learned from the holy man, and it was a huge, wonderful, staggering lesson. And it meant ... yes it meant that even he himself was a holy person somewhat.

His heart swelled and he went down the mountain path exulting, "I have seen the holy man. I have seen him."

And as he thought this, the face of the holy man did begin to form in his mind's eye like a photograph developing because even though he hadn't looked at the man, now he knew he had seen him.

In the years to come, sometimes the holy man's face would flash upon his inward eye and he would feel a catch in his throat, the pricking rush of tears to his eyes, at the sight of the beloved visage. As the years went by he felt more and more moved by his visit to the holy man which had informed his life from that day forward.

4

ANGRY MAN

One pilgrim, when the door was shut behind him, felt enraged. His blood, in a tumult, rushed to his brain, breaking blood vessels in the whites of his eyes.

He pounded on the door. He shouted at the top of his lungs, "Let me back in! You can't do this to me! Who do you think you are? You fraud! You pip-squeak!"

Angrier and angrier he grew. He banged on the door, then went down the steps, stomping on the ground, flailing his arms, looking for something to harm, to break, a rock to throw, flowers to trample, but his red eyes were too blind with rage to see a rock, a stick, a flower.

So he roared louder, calling up every vile, vicious, profane, foul word he knew, and he had many at his command, for this sort of temper tantrum was not new with him. What was new was being alone. There was no one to cower fearfully before his wrath, no one to try to placate him, shudder, turn ashen-faced, wring hands, and infuriate him further.

So his anger ran out and he began to return to his senses, but an echo was coming back to him from the hills across the valley. His words were coming back at him: Fraud! Pipsqueak! etc., but the words came not one at a time as is usually the case with echoes. No, when he fell silent, the entire vile, vicious, foul-mouthed, disgusting tirade came back to him word by word, and at the same time his shadow reenacted his insane dance, his berserk leaping, stomping, and flailing. For the first time he saw how he looked and heard how he sounded and he was ashamed.

He was a man of learning, an appreciator of the arts, a philanthropist, a leader of men, a distinguished person. He'd once been considered a sensitive person. Now he saw himself in all his brutishness, the only thing missing in the playback was his face transmogrified to gargoyle in its anger. The shadow could not give back that image, could only portray his body language, but from that he was able to imagine the rest. He was horrified. And he was cured.

Exhausted from his seizure, he sat down on a rock to rest before his descent to the town. The rock was smooth and sun-warmed. It soothed his muscles that were still twitching spasmodically from the fit.

Several round gray birds, which the holy man called boulder birds, arranged themselves in a ragged line and struck up a chorus of tweetles and trills as if for his benefit.

He felt happy and grateful. The reason he had come to see the holy man was about his temper.

5

DRUNKARD

One of the pilgrims was a drunkard. When he arrived, having come nine miles up from town, the line was a mile long. He hadn't understood the situation and so he certainly hadn't brought enough liquor to last him until he got to see the holy man. He put down the bottle he had brought, which was half gone, and asked the woman ahead of him if she would save his place in line, he had forgotten something in the town.

"No, we can't save places for people. It wouldn't be fair. No one would know how far back they were in the line if there were a lot of unknown saved places in front of them. When people arrived to fill them we would start going backwards instead of forward."

The drunk looked befuddled.

"Do you get it?" she asked.

He frowned, considered, and dimly grasped the concept, but it didn't keep him from asking other arrivals if they would save his place in line. He was a charming young man, but no matter how he cajoled and wheedled, no one agreed.

The rules of the line were: no saving (except for answering the calls of nature for which purpose shovels were available, one hundred yards away to the left or right), no bribing and, of course, not a chance of butting in.

He sipped at his bottle, trying to make it last.

The woman in front said kindly, "At some point, the line will break for the day and people will set up their camps for the night. You could go down to the town and be back in time to take your place when the line forms in the morning."

"You mean I won't get to see the holy man today?"

She laughed. "Don't you see how long the line is?"

He looked ahead. "Well, yes, it looks pretty long, but . . ."

"It isn't like a movie theater where you suddenly all go in at seven or nine o'clock. He sees us one at a time, during a part of the day. He has other things to do."

"Hmmn." He observed the line which at this time of day was in the inching-forward mode. "It looks like maybe I won't get to see him tomorrow either."

The woman laughed again.

When the line breaks, he thought, I will hurry back to town and bring enough liquor for two or, at the outside, three days. That will be heavy trucking. Why couldn't I be addicted to something lightweight, some powder or pill? It's a shame. Life is very hard. Also, we're talking eighteen miles here.

At four o'clock, the line broke and he turned and dashed down to the town, arriving at six-fifteen, making such good time that it would allow for his return before darkness, which was not until almost ten.

He went to a bar, had a few drinks, and decided not to try to go back that night; he'd go up again in the morning. It would mean being farther back in the line, but so what.

15

He woke up in the morning and besides the usual grinding headache, his quadriceps were killing him. He remembered his headlong rush down the mountain. He could hardly walk. He waited for the liquor store to open, bought three bottles, and started up the long mountain path at nine-thirty. It took him six hours, because it was steep, because of his quads, because he drank on the way and did a great deal of stumbling and backsliding the last two miles.

Now he was a lot farther down the line. He could tell because the woman he'd talked to yesterday was about a hundred yards ahead. The line broke a half hour after he arrived and while everyone set up their camps for the night, he sat down and drank.

The next day in line there was a big space at either side of the drunk because he smelled so terrible. His charm had deserted him. He made mooing, growling, or chicken-clucking sounds instead of putting words together. He was a sad case. Too bad for the people near him, but they figured he wouldn't last long.

Indeed, in two days he was out of booze again, and it dawned upon him that he'd have to make another night run. He was sober enough to realize that if he was ever going to see the holy man, he'd have to go and return in one fell swoop. No lingering in the town tavern. No spending the night at the inn. He'd better load up on food too. He'd been bumming bits of food, but it wasn't fair to the pilgrims who had to make their provisions last.

Luck was with him that the line broke earlier that day. He marked his place with a soiled handkerchief, turned, and hightailed it down the mountain. He realized he would be hard-pressed to be back before dark, and he wasn't. However, the last mile was lit by a slender moon attending the preposterous inlay of stars and, as there hadn't been time for him to drink, he was not in danger of wandering off the path or taking a serious fall.

Arriving, he lay down on his new blanket, too tired to drink, and fell into a long, sweet sleep.

Two days later, he was out of liquor again. Because of buying food, clothes, and a blanket, he hadn't had room in his pack for more than one bottle, but he'd made it last two days and nights. He began to grasp that this visit to the holy man entailed a bit more time than he'd first realized. Still, now that he knew he was capable of the run to town and back, he felt no anxiety. What's more, he was beginning to enjoy his companions even though none of them were fellow drinkers, so, when he made his next run, he offered to bring back any small necessities for his new friends.

A month later, when the door of the hermitage was opened to him, the holy man saw a muscular man with a joyful light in his clear eyes and a smile as big as a song.

"Oh, Holy One!" he said. "I'm so happy!"

He fell to his knees and kissed the hem of the small man's wheat-colored robe.

"Now, now," said the holy man. "Cut that out. Stand up and tell me about it."

He told his tale from the beginning in a rush of words, much like his rush down the mountain, because he didn't want to take too much of the holy man's time.

". . . and before I knew it, I was going to town every few days getting things for people who needed them and I wasn't buying booze at all! And I got so I could cover the distance faster and faster. You can't imagine what a quivering mass of jelly I was the first time down the mountain. It's incredible. Now I can go down in an hour and up in two! It must be a record, don't you think?"

The holy man smiled. It was almost as fast as he and his monks did it, or, to be honest, as fast as he did it up until a year or two ago.

"This is truly a wonderful story."

"That line is the best thing that ever happened to me in my life."

"I'm delighted for you. What will you do now?"

"Well ... I like doing things for people. Do you think I could be of help somewhere?"

"Almost anywhere."

By now they were at the back door. "Is there anything you want to ask me?"

"I originally came to see you because I had so many questions, but now I've forgotten them all."

"Goodbye, then, and good journey."

"Goodbye, and thank you with all my heart."

"I didn't do anything," said the holy man.

6

FEARFUL WOMAN

"Yes?"

"I've come to see the holy man."

"Please follow me."

"But I want to see the holy man."

"You've already seen me. If you will look on every-one you meet as a holy person, you will be happy. Good-bye."

So it went, day after day, rushing one person after another through the house. In. Out. Back and forth. There had been no one to talk with let alone someone to invite into his community, to take under his wing.

Normally, by the end of the summer he had gathered two or three souls to spend the winter with him, two or three who were on the path of enlightenment.

"Hello? My name is Eleanor. I hope I'm not disturbing you." She was a lovely but high-strung woman in her early thirties.

"Not at all. Please come in."

"Are you the holy man?"

"Yes I am. My name is Joe."

"How good of you to come to the door yourself. May I talk with you for just a few minutes?"

"Sit down here with me."

"Thank you so much. I'm just a poor foolish woman who doesn't deserve a moment of your time, but you see, I'm so afraid! Maybe you can help me." She clasped her hands over her breast. "I'm afraid of death."

Joe nodded understandingly.

"Not the act of dying itself but of being dead. When I think of it, I feel a complete panic, I feel such dread, such horror. It paralyzes me."

Joe nodded.

"It overshadows and dominates my life," she finished, bowing her head.

Joe said, "Because life and death are interdependent, so has your fear of death become a fear of life so that you are unable to live."

"Yes. As I sit here before you, I am as well as I've ever been because of all the fresh air and exercise I had simply in getting here. Normally I can't even leave my house."

"What you are feeling is existential anxiety and it is perfectly normal, but some people who are more sensitive than others, more creative perhaps, feel this anxiety more excruciatingly. The fear of nonbeing."

Her eyes clung hopefully to his as he spoke and her lips even moved along with his, so desperately eager was she for his help.

"And why not?" Joe said. "It is quite unacceptable that one day we will simply come to an end of our existence. But there you are. We will. It is inescapable. It is our sorry lot."

"But why can't I come to grips with it? I can't bear to suffer this ongoing terror."

"Yes, you can. Let me suggest that, when you think about nonbeing, instead of letting your mind scramble away in terror like a rat into its hole, do this."

He paused and breathed deeply. "Remain still, and calm, take deep breaths, look at your inevitable death, reflect upon it, get used to it.

"Do this every day.

"Make it a practice to dwell upon your eventual nonbeing. Gradually let it be absorbed by your courage. Yes, you have courage. We all do. But yours is currently hidden away in that same rat hole. To have our courage ready at hand we have to draw upon it regularly. We have to give it something to do."

Joe was already tired of talking and wished he was back dispensing his one sensible sentence. He was weary of the sound of his voice. He didn't believe in talking much but nor did he believe in elliptical remarks that would only leave the pilgrim puzzled and more desperate, so when he did talk he tried to be direct.

At least she was listening.

"This all sounds very difficult," she said sadly.

"It is difficult."

"I thought you would . . . well . . ."

"Make it easy? Tell you that you were going to heaven, or readying yourself for another life, or going to join the great spirit of the universe? Maybe you are.

None of us knows. We only know that we cease to exist here on earth. And yes, it will not be easy to build up your courage, but you will have a most wonderful reward right away. You will begin to enjoy your life, to use your life. Your recognition and acceptance of death—why not call it your new friendship with death—which has been established during your daily visits, will enable you to live fully."

"If I had a faith . . ."

"Yes. That can be very helpful. True faith is a blessing. However, if you throw yourself into a religion just so that your anxiety will be relieved, you will give up your freedom."

"Freedom?"

"We want to free our minds to come into harmony with the universe so as to be able to see into the true nature of things."

"Yes . . ."

"Which embracing dogma prevents. And your courage will be disappointed if it doesn't have its chance with you."

Joe stood up. She followed suit, and he escorted her to the back door. "You have started along the path. You already are a kind person. Now be courageous and, in time, be wise."

"I will try. I feel deeply inspired. Thank you with all my heart. Goodbye."

"Goodbye."

Joe watched the woman start down the precipitous path. She turned to wave, smiling a small, brave smile.

I'm not really the holy man, he thought to himself. I'm the holy chatterbox.

7

LOVERS

Joe opened the door to the lovers, who were holding hands as if inseparable. "Hello, Holy Man," they greeted him, because lovers, happy people, people who were inherently kind, seemed to have no trouble recognizing him for who he was. "We met in the line," they said of each other. "We fell in love. Isn't it wonderful? We're going to be married. Has such a thing happened here before?"

He smiled, since it happened all the time.

"Will you give us your blessing?"

"Yes."

They prepared to kneel before him, but he said, "No, don't do that. And don't bow your heads. Just look at me."

They did, beaming.

"I wish you happiness," he said. "Be kind to each other and to others. Work hard together. Keep learning about the world. When you are reading a magazine or newspaper, consider reading a novel or poetry. When reading a novel, consider reading a book on astronomy or bird behavior. Realize you have at least an extra hour every day, probably four, in which to learn a language or calculus. Use your mind to the hilt. Life passes quickly and, toward the end, gathers speed like a freight train running downhill. The more you know, the more you enrich yourselves and others."

"Thank you. We will. We'll try. And could we ask one more enormous favor? We want to name our baby after you. Could you tell us your name?"

"Joe."

This plain name seemed a paltry glory to pass on to their child, but they would make the best of it.

Each pair of lovers believed they were the only ones who had the good luck to meet and fall in love in the string of people, but the holy man couldn't count the number of new lovers who had come to his door, hands clasped together: men and women, two women or two men, young or old or mixed ages, different races or nationalities, some who couldn't speak each other's language. It was a loving, passionate line. He figured the world was already well-increased with little born or adopted Joes and Jos, offspring of the line.

As he watched the two of them set off down the path, he thought how he always forgot, in his set speech to lovers, to tell them to put the kids to bed early so they could get on with their learning. Perhaps he should send out flyers with bits of forgotten advice. He could do an air drop.

I could also urge them to think what an inspiration they will be to their youngsters who, when they start doing homework, will see their parents doing homework too!

All Joe wanted for the world was more kindness, less ignorance. This, he told his monks, was an easily achievable goal.

8

GRIEVING MAN

I have lost my wife," he told Joe when Joe invited him to sit down. "She has been taken from me. She is gone. I loved her so much. Now I will never see her again."

"Did she die?"

"Yes, that is what I am saying. She is gone."

"Well, she could have left. That would have been worse. Then you would still never see her again but have to suffer the added pain of rejection. But this is very sad. I am sorry that you had to give her back before she gave you back."

"I beg your pardon? Give her back?"

"Yes, you are adding to your grief by being such a victim. If you say to yourself that you have given her back, you will feel better. Because you see, she was never yours. Nothing that you have is yours. It never was yours."

"But that's crazy, my possessions are mine. My children are mine. And my wife . . ."

"No, they are not yours. Only you are yours. Not your possessions, not your children, not your wife. You will have to give them all back. You do not get to keep any of them."

9

FAMOUS MAN

There was a man, famous throughout the world, who particularly wanted to see the holy man. He told his point man (his personal assistant in charge of public appearances) to make all the arrangements for the visit. However, the point man was unable to contact any of the holy man's people. There was no phone or fax at the hermitage. The only mailing address was a box number in the town.

"Go to the town with the box number and work from there," said the famous man.

The point man arrived in the town below the hermitage and discovered that the road per se ended there, becoming, at the ouskirts of the town, a path called the Hermitage Trail, which purported to lead in due course to the holy man.

None of the holy man's people resided in the town, so there was no one with whom he could make arrangements for his boss's audience with him.

He called home.

"Look," said the famous man. "What do I pay you for? Go to the holy man's place yourself and make an appointment for him to see me on a certain day and I'll try to be there, although if at all possible I'd prefer for him to come and see me."

"But, sir, it's apparently ten miles up and ten miles down again. It's what they call a path. A mountain path."

"Do it."

The point man took the path. He hadn't walked farther than a city block in years. It was hard going. After a mile, he shed his coat and tie. After another mile, he loosened his shoes and his belt, and rolled up his sleeves. After the third mile he sat down and tried not to cry. His entire body was trembling. I'll never make it, he thought.

This is what I get paid for, he reminded himself.

He massaged his poor muscles, counted his woes, then steeled himself and got to his feet. At this point the path traveled alongside a fence which surrounded a pasture within which were about thirty dappled ponies.

Some men were sitting on the fence keenly observing the beasts. The point man approached them and, after such shouting, gesticulating, and waving of greenbacks, persuaded them to rent him a pony.

A pony was what he got for his money, but no saddle or bridle went with her. Still the pony seemed to know her job and trotted ebulliently up the trail, seeming to favor, even savor, the uphill which, in fact, was what she was bred for.

The point man jiggled and jounced and hung on to the thick mane and tried to keep his seat as well as keep his feet from dragging on the ground, finally figuring that a sort of lying-down arrangement on the pony's back, with his arms around the pony's neck, was the way to go—as long as no one was looking.

A walk or a canter would have been much more comfortable, but what did he know about gaits? Sometimes, for no reason he could see except that the trail allowed for it, the pony would lapse from her steady trot and go into a little sidestep-backstep dance that even included the odd pirouette, a complete whirl. It was not as if the pony was trying to dislodge him, for she seemed completely cheerful about her burden.

It was late in the day when he attained the end of the line. Of course, it was not the end of the line as he knew it—when it meant one's final destination.

What's this? he wondered.

It was evidently a large gathering of people strung out lengthwise.

He dismounted. His legs crumpled beneath him, but he recovered his footing. Even standing still, the jiggling motion did not entirely cease. He hoped the experience had not damaged his inner ear.

"Excuse me," he said, stepping on by, "I have to go on ahead to make arrangements with the holy man to see . . ." and, full of importance, he spoke the name of his boss, which was familiar to everyone within hearing.

"Oh no, you don't. You get right here at the end of the line and wait your turn like the rest of us."

The woman who spoke was similar to the woman

who confronted the drunk. It seemed that she, or someone very like her, was always near the end, keeping order,
telling newcomers what was what, sternly laying down
the law of the line. Maybe she was one of the holy man's
people placed there for that purpose, a monk in pilgrim's clothing. More likely she was simply clothed in
the robes of justice and also one who liked to be a bit
bossy, not a necessary evil but a necessary good.

"Haven't you heard of . . ." And he again uttered
the famous name.

"Yes, sure I have. And I'm impressed. Truly. But the
holy man doesn't care who is who. That doesn't mean a
thing to him."

"It might. Let me just go ahead and talk to him and
see what I can arrange. I'd be willing to pay you, and
anyone else to let me by. You can name your price."

The woman laughed. "Do you think this line is
about money? What's your problem?"

"Right now, my problem is you."

"Suppose I do decide to let you by for a thousand
dollars and so does the next person and the next person.
You've got maybe a thousand souls here . . ."

"Did you say a thousand?" He craned his neck.

"Right. So that's a thousand thousands. Help me on my math. I think it's a million. Is your boss ready to pay that?"

One thing was for sure. The point man wasn't going all the way back to the town to call his boss to find out, so he said, "Yes."

"Well, money isn't important to us." She looked pityingly upon him. "That's not why we're here."

It was one thing to pity himself, as he had been doing all day, but quite another to be pitied by this end-of-the-liner.

"Why are you here, then?" he asked.

"To find out how to live a meaningful life."

"Baby, with money you can afford all the meaning you want."

"Is money going to give you courage? Wisdom? Compassion?"

"Fast cars. Women. Beautiful houses. Respect."

"Those are what are known in the trade as unnatural and unlimited desires. They never satisfy. They do not bring happiness. You know what they bring?"

"What?"

"Despair."

"Try me." He grinned.

She fell silent.

He goaded her. "If you already know so much about what it takes: courage, wisdom, and whatever, love, I guess you said, then why bother to come all this way to the holy man?"

"To see what it looks like when it's embodied," she said, her voice trembling a little at the wonder of it, "to see that it's humanly possible."

When the line broke for the day, and people marked their spots and drifted off to be by themselves or to mingle with friends or to set up camp, the point man talked to as many of them as he could and pretty much got the same message which was: "No."

Then he saw a woman in a wheat-colored robe with a pack on her back, tripping lightly up the path. "Hey, what about her? How come she gets to go her merry way up to see the holy man?"

"Because she lives at the hermitage. She's one of the monks."

The next day, back in the town, he called his boss and told him what the deal was, described how bleak the situation, how stubborn and incorruptible the people of the line.

Then he told him about the monks. "Every few days one of them goes down the mountain to get stuff, fresh fruit and vegetables. There aren't that many of them. Maybe eight. They take turns."

"Get one of the monks to take a message to the holy man that I want to see him."

"I already tried to. She wouldn't do it. She says you have to come here and get in line like everyone else but that probably at this time of year you won't make it to the top. She says to come in the late spring and then you'll be at the front of the line. She was nice about it."

"I want to see the holy man now. Not next spring. Not next Sunday. Now. Get hold of one of the monk's robes and I'll go tripping the hell up the mountain myself. When the holy man sees that it's me, he'll understand. He'll forgive me. That's what he's all about, isn't he? Understanding? Forgiveness?" He laughed.

"Yes and he's also about courage, wisdom and compassion," the point man said.

"What the hell are you talking about? What do you

know? Just do your job and get the robe. I'm on my way."

"He's about humility," the point man said, quoting some of the other things the pilgrims had told him. "Harmony. Reason. Truth. . . ." But the famous man had already hung up.

10

VIOLENCE

The point man nabbed the next monk who came to town, which was four days later. Getting a steely grip on his arm, he led him unprotestingly to his room at the inn. His boss had already arrived and was ensconced in a separate suite.

The point man telephoned him. "I got a monk," he said.

"Be right there."

The famous man came in. "I'm sorry about this," he said. "I've got to borrow your robe to see the holy man. I promise you he'll understand when he sees who I am."

"Who are you?"

He told the point man to tell the monk who he was. "Maybe your friend should steal a robe too," the monk said, "so as to be with you when you arrive and tell the holy man who you are when he asks."

"Don't be a wise guy," the point man said reprovingly. "Take off your robe. Strip. Let's get this over with." He was sweating and uncomfortable. He didn't like this one bit.

The monk did not take off his wheat-colored robe.

"Get the robe," the famous man said, quickly shedding his own clothes down to his underwear.

The point man stepped forward but could go no farther. He simply was not going to undress the monk. To his own astonishment, he discovered there was a line he wouldn't cross and this was it. He wouldn't do it. Not for any amount of money.

He told this to the famous man, who said, "Then you're fired."

"I don't care."

The point man sat down in a chair and mopped his

brow while the famous man said, "Come on, old fellow, let's get this over with." He stepped forward, leaned down, grabbed the hem, and started pulling the robe up over the monk's body. But the monk would not obligingly raise his arms. So the famous man grit his teeth, raised his hand, and struck him down.

The famous man was able to free the robe from the body of the half-conscious monk.

He pulled on the clean, soft, cotton robe, which came to a little below his knees.

"I'm sorry, but I just had to see the holy man," he told the fallen monk who lay still, blood dripping from his nose.

The man on the floor decided that this was one time when he wouldn't say to the pilgrim, "You have already seen me."

The walk would be good for the famous man, Joe thought fuzzily. The reception he'd get at the hermitage would be very good for him. And the return walk down the mountain in his jockey shorts would be the best. The monks would see that he went down the way he had come, past the people waiting in line. That would make a better man of him and he would be more famous than ever, a thousand times more famous.

Of course, he thought more fuzzily, the sad likeli-hood is that I will have to go *up* the mountain in my un-derpants. Still I shall have the privacy of the back side, the un-pilgrimmed trail.

When the famous man left, the point man raised the small monk from the floor and set him gently on the bed. He washed the blood from his face and stayed by the bed, watching over him.

He resolved to carry the monk, if need be, back to the monastery or whatever it was called. Yes, he who could barely make it halfway up on his own two feet would carry the man, would crawl on his hands and knees and let him ride on his back if necessary, to bring him safely home.

The point man knelt by the bed with his hands clasped, his head bowed, face washed by continuously running tears, feeling unutterable remorse for having participated in such a loathsome deed as battering this poor, small, old monk who hadn't looked so old or small while standing there refusing to relinquish his robe but was now revealed to be very old and small in-deed.

Joe couldn't tell him to get up off his knees because he had drifted off to a healing sleep.

11

KINDNESS

The holy man did not have to go up the hill in his underpants and the point man did not have to carry him.

In an hour, he awoke refreshed, said he was feeling just fine and could he please borrow some clothes.

The point man gave him a pair of designer jeans and a red polo shirt. He wanted to give him everything he owned, including all his money, but the monk told him thanks but all he needed was the clothes.

"You will want your money. Don't forget, you've lost your job."

"I've lost everything, including my self-respect."

"Just continue being as kind to people as you have been to me and you will be a happy man."

"Really? Is it that simple?"

"Yes."

"But what did I do exactly?"

You took care of me, a complete stranger. You bathed my wounds and watched over my sleep. You prayed for me. You offered me all that you had."

"That's right I did. That's kindness, eh? I guess you could call it love too." He ventured, "Compassion?"

"Yes."

"Courage?"

"You showed courage standing up to your boss, risking all."

The point man was brightening by the minute, but then he said sorrowfully, "I should have protected you from him. I should never have let this horrible thing happen in the first place."

"It was my fault. But I think some good has come of it. I wish you well. Goodbye."

Years later, both living good lives in utter obscurity, the ex-point man would encounter his ex-boss and learn from him that the little monk was the holy man.

"He wore my clothes!" he would tell his ex-boss, thrilled.

"I wore *his* clothes!" was the abashed but equally thrilled reply. He added, "Nothing ever felt so soft or smelled so sweet."

12

THE ROBE

The holy man had learned the language of the country. After purchasing supplies he kept a doctor's appointment, then went to the park and played with the children. He sorely missed children up at the hermitage. They ran to him, greeting him happily. He played ball with them, wrestled, and rolled down the grassy hill. They played hide-and-seek among the many-tentacled banyan trees, then enjoyed a long silent period in which they sat together listening to each other breathe, a scene the mothers, fathers, and nannies found awesome and inexplicable.

Then he started up the mountain, sticking with

his decision to take the back path so that the pilgrims would not be upset by the sight of some buttinski forging ahead, one who did not wear the distinguishing robe.

It was a beautiful day. He felt happy, free, so glad to be out and about. Now that he was older, or, face it, old, his friends at the hermitage were growing terribly protective of him and weren't inclined to let him do his share of the supply-getting. They didn't like him going off alone, were afraid that something might happen to him, that he might have a fall or, who knows, a heart attack.

He smiled. Come to think of it, they were right, something had happened to him; he'd been knocked unconscious and stripped of his robe. Now his friends would be impossible in their concern. And yet they knew as well as he himself that one couldn't live with fear or one wasn't living at all. And worry was beneath contempt. What a waste of reason.

It was up to him, not them, to look out for himself. Not to fall. To step carefully. Pick up his feet. Be attentive. What happened this morning was his fault because he hadn't given up the robe.

He walked through the Woods of Clattering Leaves, as he called it, which was mostly ginkgo trees. Joe had taught himself the names of flora and fauna, but now he liked to make up names of his own. Here, because of the cascade and waterfall, there was always a breeze stirring the leaves of the deciduous trees, hence the clattering sound.

Why hadn't he relinquished the robe? he asked himself. He was surprised at his stubborn behavior. Why had he not raised his arms and allowed it to be whipped away or, better still, simply taken it off himself and given it to the man who wanted it so terribly badly?

What was his attachment to his robe?

He was not ashamed of his old body. Certainly it was not as pretty as it once was. The skin was dry and slack and hung in folds. His limbs had shrunk. Even his member was diminished. His legs were bowed as if he'd been a perpetual cowboy. But he didn't care. His body wasn't him and he had no more control over its aging than he did of his death, come when it may.

One simply let go of things beyond one's control, didn't trouble about them, didn't let them bow one down.

He did miss the unconfined feeling of the robe, the air on his legs. He'd forgotten the discomfort of pants.

Now he had reached the pasture of stumpy-legged, dappled ponies and so he climbed on the fence to watch them being put through their paces, waving to other fence-sitting equine observers on the other side.

There was a game in progress, similar to polo. The difference was the riders rode bareback and reinless, the horses responding to signals from their knees and heels. Uniquely, the field of play was steep, not flat, and the only goal was at the upward end. There was no downward end. The ball, if it eluded the sweeping mallets, could roll downhill for miles.

Joe was a keen fan of the game, too keen, and only allowed himself a few minutes (well, ten) before forcing himself off the fence and back on the trail. He walked briskly on to where the path diverged—Hermitage Trail and Back Trail, taking the back one.

After five more miles, he stopped, set down his pack, and looked about. He viewed the valley below, the hills beyond outlined in layers against the horizon. Cirrus and cumulus patterned the sky like giant Japanese characters, cloud haiku. Around him were wild grasses, flowers, scattered rocks. Insects were everywhere and a mockingbird, blown from its normal flight pattern, virtually lost on an unknown mountain, perched itself on the limb of an altitude-stunted tree and sang joyously, not knowing the meaning of anxiety.

There were masses of blue flowers resembling pieces of fallen sky, releasing only a faint scent as if their main thrust was color.

He leaned down to one of the ubiquitous springs and drank deeply. Then he plucked a yellow apple from his pack and thanked nature and the hands of men and women for providing it before biting into it. It was a good apple.

He lay back, enjoying the warm sun on his skin.

He was glad that the many people who came to see him were experiencing this too. Most of them probably never had climbed a mountain or slept under the stars. He wished everyone in the world could have such a celestial vacation, get back in touch with earth and sky.

He watched a raven and a red-tailed hawk soar in tandem, performing sensational aerial stunts as if to challenge the other's winged skill. Joe was unable to judge the winner, never having flown himself.

He lost the flight-masters in the sun, closed his eyes, and reflected some more on the question of the be-grudged robe—his not relinquishing it.

But it no longer interested him.

What was done was done.

And good had come of it. If the famous man hadn't struck him down, the point man wouldn't have come to his understanding of how to be.

And probably right about now the famous man, wending his way downhill in his jockey shorts, was com-ing to an understanding too.

13

PUNISHMENT

The famous man left the town and bounded up the mountain. He was in good shape, a tennis player and jogger. Still, by mile five he quit bounding and walked. After all, no one was watching. He hit a good stride and when he began passing the pilgrims in their camps he still walked vigorously but only because he was forcing himself. The last two miles were the steepest and he would have dearly loved to stop and catch his breath, maybe even sit down for a while, but he didn't want to have to talk to anyone and so pressed on.

He looked silly in the robe that came only to his knees. He had tied a yellow scarf around his head to cover his famous hair and look more like a monk, but this only added to his bizarre appearance.

The pilgrims smiled and laughed at the strange, long-legged, be-kerchiefed monk but had to admire him for not seeming to care what a figure he cut.

He arrived at the hermitage. When his knock was unanswered, he walked on in and found the dining room where seven men and women in wheat-colored robes, all with shaved heads, were eating their lunch in silence.

These people were friends of Joe's whom he had known when he lived in the world, or who had sought him out in recent years and become close to him, those specially enlightened ones he had chosen from among the pilgrims.

Every year these or other friends came and spent the summer with him. This summer the group consisted of a scientist named Maria, a cellist named Ho, Henri, a lawyer, Kim, a young marathoner, a chef named Helena, Ed, who was a poet, and Daniel, a dancer. They were all high achievers, some almost as famous as the famous man. Joe encouraged everyone to live to their fullest potential, understanding that it was devotion to one's work or art or sport that led to accomplishment and personal fulfillment while also contributing to the world's progress. In the fall, they would return to their own countries and to their work, with their minds sharpened and their hearts full.

In the meantime, they shaved their heads and wore the same robes so as to have the spirit of community.

Their day, which was spent in complete silence, began with some hours of meditation, or prayer, or reflection, then breakfast and indoor/outdoor chores, which this summer included putting on a new roof. The afternoon was given over to their own personal work, practice, or study.

After dinner, they gathered in the common room and talked together. Sometimes there was a performance from the cellist, poet, or dancer, a talk from one of the others.

That is who they were but what the famous man saw were seven, humble, bald monks whom he imagined were there in residence only to see to the needs of the holy man. They might have been the Seven Dwarfs for all he cared.

He mistook their grave, horrified looks for astonishment at his uncelebrated appearance in their midst.

"Yes, it's me," he said, removing the scarf to expose his glorious hair. "You can believe your eyes, folks. You're not seeing things. I know it's pretty amazing. Yes, I walked up the mountain. All by myself. What?"

They were pointing at him and he accordingly looked down at himself.

"The robe? You're wondering about the robe? Well, you see . . . Do you speak English, by the way?"

One of them nodded. They were all beginning to get to their feet. "Oh, please, don't get up. Actually, I wouldn't mind sitting down with you. I could use something to eat and drink myself." He coughed as if to demonstrate the dryness of his throat.

One of them put his hands on the robe.

"Oh, yes, the robe. You see, I had to get right up here to see the holy man and, because there's absolutely no way to get hold of him, I did the only thing I could which was to take the robe from your little friend down in the town. That allowed me free passage up the trail."

The monks were aghast.

"No harm done, I assure you. The holy man will understand when I explain . . . if you'll only let me see him. My time is damned precious." The famous man was beginning to lose patience with the mute, inhospitable monks.

"Don't you guys ever say anything? What do you want? The robe? You want the robe off my body? Okay, take it easy. No problem."

Unlike Joe, the famous man was not averse to lifting his arms in the air although he did have a momentary flash of feeling under arrest.

"Have you got something else I can put on? I'd really like something to wear when I see the holy man. Don't tell me one of you guys is the holy man."

They began to physically herd him down the hall to the front door. The words "bum's rush" came to mind.

"Wait a minute, this is the door I came in by. I didn't come all the way up here to be treated like this and on top of it all not even see the holy man. Or get a bite to eat," he couldn't help but add. "Do you know who I am? Maybe you didn't recognize me after all."

They looked so angry with him that he decided not to pursue the topic of his identity. It was hard to have a rational discussion with folks who remained silent and glowering. But their obvious enmity made him nervous. Now words like "mob mentality" came to mind. He saw all the stones littered around the front yard, and it occurred to him that if one monk cast a stone at him, all the others would follow suit.

If only he could talk to the man in charge. "Holy Man?" he started calling loudly in his famous voice that was mellifluous even in its shouting form. "Hello? I'm here! Your crummy minions are preventing me from seeing you."

The monk who had the robe held it up in the air at the level it would be were Joe inside of it.

"You're not trying to tell me it's the holy man's robe, are you? No. Oh no. Say it isn't so. If it's so, I'll kill myself."

They closed the door in his face as if to say that sounded like a good idea to them.

I am the biggest jerk that ever walked on the face of the earth, the man thought. I will never be able to look at myself in the mirror, let alone stand up in front of the cameras.

It had only taken him a minute to go from wanting

to kill himself to vowing not to look in the mirror so much.

He did not think of the holy man and his side of it during his stumbling descent past the pilgrims; he thought only of himself and his embarrassment, which was perhaps natural with all the laughter and the hooting.

He realized that after the pilgrims had enjoyed their belly laughs they would animatedly discuss his buoyant ascent and cowed descent and put together the story of the stolen robe since he had returned so soon from the hermitage dressed only in his underpants.

Then the whole world would learn the story—if the world hadn't already learned the worst of it from the fired point man.

He would have to go into hiding until it blew over. But it would never blow over. He would have to change his identity. He would have to give up everything.

It seemed awfully harsh punishment for one stupid impulsive act that it should get him in hot water with seven monks and expose him (literally) to a thousand people and end by him having to wipe himself off the face of the earth.

What if he faced the music and told the story himself. Or got his people to put some spin on it . . . But no, it was totally untellable. Even if he altered it, embellished it, there was no way he would come out smelling like a rose. He'd knocked out the holy man and robbed him of his robe, so as to put it on and go see the holy man.

Even then he didn't think about the small man he had brutally struck down, didn't wonder if he had hurt him or if he was all right.

It was enough, more than he could handle, to wonder what the world was going to think about him.

He would have to disappear, the quicker the better.

During the long disconsolate return to town his inflation seeped away like a pinprick releasing air from a very large balloon. He saw that his behavior had become callous in the extreme and his attack on the monk that morning was not unusual for him and that, had it not been the holy man, he wouldn't have thought twice about it, let alone considered going into hiding because of it.

He tried to think back to when his heartlessness had begun.

14

EGO

What do you think he came to see you about?" the monks wondered aloud that evening.

"His egotism," answered Maria, the scientist, laughing. "He wanted a stronger ego."

They all laughed but Joe said, "You are right. When he grows stronger in his ego he will no longer be so egotisical."

"Aren't we supposed to abandon our egos?" Maria asked.

"Yes. When your ego gets strong enough you will be able to slough it off."

"If I abandoned my ego, what would happen to my science?"

"Einstein completely abandoned his ego," said Joe. "Then he was free to think, free to release his intuitive power."

"He had his devoted assistant to protect him. I think without an ego you need someone to look after you."

"Do you think I need someone to take care of me?" Joe asked.

"Yes," she said.

"Absolutely," they all said, laughing and pointing to his black eyes and puffed-up nose.

15

IMPATIENT
WOMAN

The long line to the holy man, if
seen from above by an alien, could be construed to be
one organism, for when the top end of it moved, the
ripple of movement passed along the entire body. Indeed, each individual felt such a connection to the line,
so bonded to the persons at either side of him, that it
was almost hard to disband when the word came from
the hermitage that the holy man had stopped receiving
for the day.

It was amazing too how word traveled like lightning
up and down the line, any little drama that had tran-

spired among pilgrims, any accident, or love affair, or illumination—it belonged to them all, because they were the line.

They were individual pilgrims from all over the world, but they were also one entity, with a strong solidarity. If it was threatened, or seemed threatened, by the occasional troublemaker, crazy person, or desperate person, alarm spread through its body.

All pilgrims had to be integrated, but there were those ones who could make the line feel anxious, unhappy, vulnerable to harm, so that the experience of being in the line, which in itself was so healing, could be blighted. At these times, the line felt imperiled so that, if seen from above, it seemed to bristle, squirm, release an ominous cloud into its atmosphere.

The impatient woman arrived early in the year when the line was not very long, maybe two hundred yards, but it looked long to her.

"This is ridiculous," she said. "Why, it's not even moving."

"He hasn't begun seeing people yet today," said the man ahead of her. "When he does, it moves pretty fast."

"And meanwhile, you just stand here."

"That's right."

The woman stood a few more minutes, fidgeting. She asked what hours the holy man saw people and the man said it varied. Usually between the hours of nine and twelve in the morning, but sometimes between one and four in the afternoon.

"He only receives us during three hours of the day! That's terrible. This should be better organized. And look, it's twenty past nine now and we might as well be stuck in cement, so it's probably going to be the afternoon hours today, right?"

He shrugged.

"Well," she announced, "I'm not going to wait around any longer."

"It's up to you."

She turned and started back down the trail, glad to be doing something, made momentarily stupid by her impatience, deprived of reason by her overriding exasperation. However, she soon realized that the hours it would take her to walk down would be the hours, if she stayed, she'd be moving up in the line when the line started to move, which could be any minute.

Not to mention the fact that, if she departed, she would not see the holy man at all.

This gave her pause and she stopped. She fell into an agony of indecision, stepping first forward, then backward, much like the dance of the dappled ponies.

Ahead of her she saw some people coming up the path. If she was not quick to turn, they would take her abandoned place in the line.

"Don't bother coming," she called out to them. "The line's too long. And it's not even moving."

They disregarded her advice and passed her by. There went her place.

I spent several days getting here, she told herself reasonably. I should be willing to spend another day waiting.

But it's so hard. Getting here I was in motion. It's the standing around that's so maddeningly difficult, just standing there with my face hanging out, not doing anything. I didn't bring anything to read, or sew. I wonder if anyone has a crossword puzzle book or a pack of cards. Well, there's always charades.

She turned and hurried back up the path to the line and took her place behind the two people who had passed her.

"Change your mind?"

"Yes. I'm afraid I'm very restless. It's hard for me to be still."

The man kindly taught her how to breathe slowly and deeply from the abdomen, concentrating on a long out-breath, letting the in-breath take care of itself.

"It will relax you," he said.

It wasn't a crossword puzzle, but it was something with which to pass the time. She was a quick learner, a perfectionist, and pretty much excelled at all she undertook to do. But she was one who had never found out that thing to do with her life which would fully occupy her and satisfy her restlessness. This was why she had come to see the holy man.

In no time at all she was a champion deep-breather, but this, of course, was not a career choice.

The line didn't move much that day. When it broke for the camp-making, she went about talking to people with the idea of reorganizing the system.

"Why not take turns? One day, the men could stand in line, another day, the women. That way they'd be free to take walks or go back to town to make phone calls or do anything they wanted.

"Or why not figure out exactly how many people, at

most, the holy man could see in three hours and just those people stand in the line for that day?

"Or there could be a watchman assigned to stand at the head of the line and signal when the holy man began to receive the pilgrims so we could all fall into place. Or . . ."

They told her that her ideas were impractical—mainly because there were always new people arriving. They pointed out the three main rules: no bribing, no saving places, no butting in. They said that, as it was, there were rule-breakers and troublemakers. If they tried anything new it would be anarchy. The line actually worked very well as it was. Nor would her ideas move the line along any faster.

Her ears pricked up when told of the existence of troublemakers, not considering for a minute that she herself, in a minor way, was well-ensconced in that category.

She said that she worked in the justice system (which was a lie) and it would be her pleasure to solve any problems that came up in the line and to keep order in general. She was very good at that sort of thing, and it would keep her busy while she waited to see the holy man. She was absolutely longing for something to do "or," said she, "I'll go mad."

She told everyone to please send word up or down the line if she was needed.

Not wanting the newcomer to go mad, they kept her busy with any problems that arose in the line.

When she went to help, she lost her place and had to begin again at the end because the strict rules applied to her as well. But it was worth it to her to lose her spot if it meant having something to do.

In this way, the one who was most impatient to see the holy man never got to see him because she was always going to the end of the line. Day after day she made absolutely no progress, no headway. If anything, her movement was downward and backward.

That was all right with her. She didn't mind because she was busy and useful and needed. It was she who confronted the drunk and tried to straighten out the point man.

At first she would scramble and scurry to where she was summoned, anxious to get to the job but, over time, she began to move slower and to get there just as fast, arriving serene and unruffled so that her very calmness eased the problem. She met a lot of people and made many friends. She stayed the entire summer.

At the end of the summer there ceased to be new arrivals and the line grew shorter every day. It looked like she was going to get to see the holy man at last. But she decided she would rather come back to see him next year when there would be a whole new line to need her managing and counseling abilities. Meanwhile she would seek out other kinds of lines.

She had found her career in life: Line Master.

Sometimes in her secret heart of hearts she called herself Peacemaker.

16
RIVALS

There was one woman in the line who was so intent on getting to the holy man that she could not think of anything else. She paid no attention to the other pilgrims but only concentrated on the movement upwards as if by an exercise of will she would get there quicker. When the line broke for the day, she went off alone as if talking to others would only distract her from her mission and maybe abort it. She was eager to look over any newcomers, however, just as she'd been concerned, upon arriving, to study the people who were ahead of her.

Her name was Marion. Because she came early in the year, she was able to reach the hermitage door in only six days.

When Joe told her who he was as he was ushering her out, her eyes glittered with victory. I did it! she thought, and couldn't wait to get back home to tell her friend.

This look of Aha! did not escape the holy man.

"Did you want to ask me something?"

"No, not really. I just wanted to see you."

"That's what I thought. Let me ask you something then. What is the opposite of love?"

"Hate, of course."

"No, it is envy."

His words did not particularly sink in. She was in too much of a rush to get home and had a long way to go. She only thought, glancingly, don't talk to me about envy. I am not envious. It is Winnie who is so envious. Envy, indeed!

Marion and her friend Winnie had been rivals since girlhood. It began by being a normal, friendly rivalry—who had the cutest boyfriend, the prettiest dress—then it evolved to who could marry the richest man and, that accomplished, have the biggest house, the finest car.

But anyone could buy things.

The rivalry refined itself to which of them could have the most interesting guest to dinner. That kept them busy for years. Because they were provincial women, they weren't playing in the big leagues, so neither one's dinner table was ever graced by a person of international or even national eminence, but Winnie got a state senator once and Marion a college president.

Down through the years it was always who could have the most wonderful vacation at the most glamorous resort, which evolved in time to who could discover the most out-of-the-way vacation and finally evolved, or disintegrated, into who could have the most demanding, strenuous, and wretchedly miserable vacation, such as running a marathon or river, crossing deserts and polar ice caps.

Over the years, nobody won, although there were fleeting triumphs.

Then Marion heard about the holy man. (By now both women were widows and heading toward old age.) She prayed with all her heart that Winnie didn't know about him yet, or if she did, it hadn't entered her mind to try and see him. This would be a real coup. This would be the *crème de la crème* of accomplishments. Winnie would be green with envy, would be utterly defeated once and for all.

Marion made her plans in secret and took off for the faraway town at the foot of the mountain. Her quest was successful except for those rankling words the holy man had bestowed upon her in parting.

When she got home she did not at once tell Winnie where she had been. She was waiting for the perfect moment when poor Winnie would throw up some piddling triumph to her and she could forthwith crush her with her paramount deed of having climbed the mountain to see the holy man.

She waited in vain because Winnie was no longer acting spiteful and jealous, no longer seeking to impress. She was actually being quite nice.

Marion began to suspect that Winnie too had seen the holy man and that she too was waiting for the perfect moment to annihilate her with the news.

Or else Winnie had seen the holy man and changed thereby, had gotten some message from him, maybe the same message, maybe a different one, and become the lovely person that she seemed to be now.

Well, Marion would show her. She was going to be

an even nicer person. She went out and did good works and made a name for herself as a charitable woman. She was a familiar at all fund-raisers, soup kitchens, settlement houses, and rehabilitation centers. She made sure her picture got in the paper so that Winnie would know.

Then she found out Winnie was also doing good works, only quietly.

There was only one thing left. Marion decided to sell everything she owned and give it all to the poor. This took some while and in the meantime Winnie disappeared.

She has probably gone to India to work with Mother Teresa, Marion thought crossly. Well, good riddance to her. I'm still giving all my money to the poor. What do I want with this big old house anyway?

Deep down in her heart, however, she felt very sad to think that she might have lost her old friend, that she might never see her again.

But Marion found Winnie living at the same boarding house she moved into. She told her how happy she was to find her, that she had missed her and that she loved her.

"I love you too," Winnie said. "Isn't it wonderful

not to live with envy anymore but instead to feel love for each other?"

Aha! Just as I suspected! Marion thought. And it was on the tip of her tongue to say, I saw the holy man too, you know. But she didn't because what if by some slim chance she was wrong and Winnie never had gone to see him? It would crush her.

17

JEALOUS MAN

He was the last customer of the day. When Joe led him to the back door and said good-bye, the pilgrim protested, "But I haven't seen the holy man!"

"Yes, you have seen me," Joe said.

"My dear fellow, I'm terribly sorry. I had no idea. Forgive me."

"Don't mention it. However, if from now on you will treat everyone that you meet like a holy person, you will be happy."

"I will certainly try to do that. Although until now

I have seen little evidence to encourage me to think of people being holy."

"Nor did you see it now," the holy man reminded him.

"Er . . . quite right. So the idea is to go on the assumption of intrinsic holiness and be a happier man for proceeding along those lines. Yes, I see. And if I am wrong . . ."

"You will not be wrong. We are all holy."

"All God's creatures great and small, so to speak . . ."

"If it helps to speak of it that way." Joe was still standing with the door open. "Goodbye."

"But please! Now that I have your ear, could I seek your advice on my problem?"

"Fire away."

"I am married to a lovely, intelligent, wonderful woman and I am consumed by jealousy about her. I am constantly imagining that she is unfaithful to me. I am jealous of her friends, her time, the air she breathes, the clothes on her back. It is not that I have nothing else to do or to think about. I am an inventor and work very hard.

"We live far out in the country, and I always know

exactly where she is and who she's with, for we have a car phone and she is required by me to carry a phone on her person and, of course, I think nothing of having her followed.

"She goes along with all this for the sake of keeping the peace and because she truly loves me despite my infuriating obsession. Even though I treat her like a virtual prisoner I know that if she wanted a lover she would have one. Women can always find ways, can't they?"

He seemed to be waiting for an answer, so Joe said, "Yes."

"Exactly. So I put myself in her mind and stay one step ahead of her. I know in my heart she doesn't want a lover, but then I think, maybe I am driving her to it."

He went on in this vein until Joe, perhaps wishing his last customer would not prolong closing time indefinitely, asked him, "Given this desperate situation, how were you able to leave the poor woman for such a long time?"

"One day I went to her room (not knocking on the door so as to surprise her in whatever suspicious action she might be engaged in) and I found her standing before the mirror with a knife in her hands. Horrified, I figured I'd driven her to suicide or murder, but it was neither. She said she was going to disfigure herself. Then I would have nothing to be jealous about.

"I promised her I would cease badgering her and get help. A friend told me about you, so I came. I have been in the line a month and it has been wonderful. My phone cannot reach her from this mountain so I have simply had to trust her. As a result, I have been released from the clutches of the green-eyed monster. For the first time in years I am free and at peace. I am sure the peace and freedom she is feeling is stupendous. But now I am afraid to go home.

"Holy Man, the burning question is, can I maintain these peaceful feelings, or will the torment start up again upon my return?"

"Tell me what you have learned."

"I guess I've learned that trust brings peace."

"Good. What if you go home and trust her and she betrays you?"

"Well, that will be horribly painful. Maybe it will kill me, but still, I won't have driven her to it, and we will have had a time of peace. I can't help it if she betrays me. It will be up to her. I can control myself, but I can't control her. That is something else I have learned."

"Wonderful. And there is one more thing you have learned which will make all the difference in carrying out your new program."

He looked blank.

"It is about how you are going to treat her."

Joe waited while the man thought over their exchange, then watched as he smiled happily and exclaimed, "Yes. I remember. I'm going to treat her with honor and kindliness, as an equal, and listen to what she says and believe her—just like I would treat you."

18

THE QUESTION

Four women pilgrims who had become friends in the line sat around their campfire talking. Liv was a woman in her early sixties, from Scandinavia, a maternal and successful woman, to whom the others were naturally drawn.

"When I send my grandchildren gifts, they do not write me thank-you notes," she said.

The others nodded. There was nothing new about that old problem.

"It makes me so sad. That's why I have come to see the holy man, to ask him what to do."

The others sat up with dropped jaws, quite shocked at this admission.

"But Liv, honey, that's the sort of question in our country we write to an advice column about. We don't spend all this time and money coming to see the holy man who, in any case, I can assure you, is into much deeper matters."

They all began to laugh at Liv and her question. "You might as well ask him how to get children to pick up their clothes."

A man moved into their firelight from the shadows, a jolly person who was another favorite among them. "I'm behind you all the way, Liv. This is a question that has baffled western civilization."

Another man said, "I think I can tell you what the holy man will say. The answer is that you are bringing this suffering upon yourself, and in order to relieve yourself of it, you can do one of two things. You can stop sending them presents. Or you can just be happy with the giving and not expect or hope for a thank-you note, the idea being that if you don't hope, you won't be disappointed."

"Well," Liv admitted, "sometimes I have stopped

sending presents, for a while. But I have more money than they do, and they need the clothes and the fun things they wouldn't have otherwise. I'm sure you're right about the hoping. I think I have taught myself not to expect the letters, but I still feel so hurt when I don't get them."

Others crowded around the fire. "I sacrificed and went without to send my son to college. It cost me eighty thousand dollars. He never thanked me."

"Most kids take it for granted that you'll pay for their education," said one of the women. "Like it's part of their birthright."

"Maybe grandchildren think the same way," a woman suggested helpfully. "They expect ongoing presents from their grandma. It's a given, a part of life."

"Do you talk to them on the phone?" Liv was asked.

"Sometimes I call to ask them if they got the presents and they thank me and say they really like them. But I want them to tell me without my calling to ask. I want them to write to me, on their own."

"I don't see why you didn't spend this money going to see them instead of the holy man. That way they could get to know you."

"Except for this year, I have gone every summer to spend a month with them," Liv said. "I have my own business, so I am able to take the time. I stay at a nearby inn because my daughter-in-law is not so fond of me and I don't feel comfortable in her house."

The other women muttered darkly at this.

"My son is not a perfect husband to her and she blames me. She says I spoiled him and now I am spoiling the grandchildren."

More dark muttering.

"I always have a good visit with the children and when I go away I am sure that they will write me thank-you notes when I next send them presents, but they never do."

"My daughter lives two thousand miles from me," said a woman. "I used to send her money for her college education. She never wrote to me unless I was a little late with the money. After a couple of years, I began to be suspicious. I investigated and found out she wasn't going to college. She was living with a man and supporting him."

They all gasped. "What a betrayal!"

"My son died," said another. "It was a freak accident. He was running and he jumped over a fence and misjudged. He caught his foot and landed flat, hitting his head on a rock. He was in a coma for a long time and then he died, my darling boy."

She wiped tears away and others did too.

By now a lot of people had joined their circle around the fire and two others offered stories of losing their children—one to suicide, another to drugs, and so forth.

Liv's problem grew more and more insignificant in the light of these terrible tragedies.

But not to her.

During the ensuing days she became an object of mirth to many in the line—the woman who had come to ask the holy man how to get her grandchildren to write thank-you notes to her.

One day the jolly man asked her, "Do you think that if they wrote to you it would prove that they love you?"

She thought about it. "Yes, I guess that's it. It would prove I was in their minds, that I had some reality in their life. I feel so alone. My husband is dead. In not so many years, I will follow him. I want them to remember me. But how can they if they do not even remember me when I am alive?"

The man frowned and shook his head. It was a sorry situation, all right. He didn't have an answer. But he was one who always looked on the bright side so he said, "Maybe they will miss you this summer, be so disappointed you didn't come visit that everything will change."

She lit up. "That's what I was hoping, but I didn't dare admit it to myself. Maybe right now they are wishing with all their hearts that I was with them and vowing to do differently concerning me, vowing to show their appreciation."

"Let's hope so," he said warmly, not realizing he was disregarding the other man's advice about the perils of hoping or expecting.

In her heart, though, Liv feared they didn't care or, worse, didn't notice, that their grandmother hadn't come to see them this summer.

Two days later she was able to lay out her trouble to the holy man, detaining him at the back door after he told her who he was, grasping his sleeve and not letting go until she had emptied her heart.

"Egotism!" he said sternly so that she dropped his sleeve as if burnt and fell back against the door. "You are suffering from an advanced case of egotism," he admonished, going overboard as he was sometimes wont to do. "I can tell you right now that if they each wrote you ten pages a week you would not be satisfied, would still feel wronged and unappreciated and probably want twenty pages! How can those children love you until you are able to love them? Selflessly. Unconditionally. Goodbye."

As the door closed behind her and she started down the mountain path, the long, lonely path so conducive to reflection, she exclaimed aloud, "The very idea! Who does he think he is? Well, I never! He's obviously never had ungrateful children to deal with, living his rarefied life as he does. What does he know about giving, giving, giving, and getting no return?"

Then she thought how he gave of himself every day of his life and there was no donation box, no plate being passed, no beautifully printed, carefully worded requests for money in the mail. He had not written any books for them to buy nor were there any relics: holy man pictures, splinters of hermitage, chips of surrounding boulders, small bottles of holy man spring water.

Flushing, she remembered him saying that if they wrote ten pages she would expect twenty, and she began to admit to herself that she had sometimes received certain scrawls and scribbles from her grandchildren over the years but had discounted them, telling herself that their mother or father had made them write to her. Was that what he meant by never being satisfied?

But, my goodness, isn't it natural for a mother or grandma to want to be loved and appreciated? I really do not in the least see what's so egotistical about that.

She remembered all the many times, hundreds of times over the years, she had said to her grandchildren, "Do you love your grandma?" But she could not remember saying "I love you" to them.

Yes, she began to see and began to feel free from herself, to feel her heart lift. She sat down on a rock to look at the view and to look at the new life that was unfolding within her.

She heard footsteps and, looking back, saw that her three women friends, having waited for each other, were hurrying down the path after her.

"We are dying to know what the holy man told you," they said.

Shame smote her. She bowed her head. It was hard for her to speak. It was like admitting she had a horrible disease. She tried.

"What?" they urged her. "What?"

Her chin knocked against her collar bone. "He said I was a terrible egotist."

They fell silent, as shocked by his answer as they had originally been by her question. But they were reluctant to sympathize. The holy man must know the truth of the matter. They began to feel somehow impressed, as if she'd been favored. He must have really cared—to tell her such a thing, to not pull his punches.

"Nevertheless, you are a holy person," said the youngest woman, surprising Liv, who looked up to see who she was talking about.

"Yes, you. Now that he has told you that you are an egotist, you don't need to be one any more. You can be holy. As we all are. If we treat everyone as a holy person, we will be happy. He told us so."

"Is that so?" said Liv to the ebullient youngster. "How long will it take?"

"It's instant. I feel that I am a holy person right now and that you are too and that is that. It's that simple. He said it was so and it is so. Let's not make a big deal out of it." She laughed. She had embraced with ardor the idea of treating everyone as a holy person and couldn't wait to get going—which was why she got going on Liv. And it worked. Already she felt happier and Liv looked happier too.

They hugged each other and went down the hill together.

Liv felt light-hearted going down the path with her friends. It's going to be fun, she thought, not being egotistical. She hadn't felt like this since she was a child. She felt a new life beginning, one that was full of possibilities.

Yes! She would be forgiving to her grandchildren, to every one, and be a nobler person all around, a person people would look up to as they did to the holy man, look up to and learn from.

Unfortunately, Liv began to feel important in her new role as holy person. She held her head high, trying out a benign smile, wishing she had a mirror.

"Wait for me!"

They turned and saw the jolly person running after them. "What did he say to you? What is the answer to the celebrated thank-you note question?"

Liv, again, had difficulty speaking the dread word but her three friends assisted her, shouting, "Egotism!"

"I see," said the man. "Yes, well, of course children are bound to be egotistical. It is the nature of being a child. They are busy with their friends and their games. And their worries. Kids have worries, too. It's not easy being a kid. Or an adult either. I don't know which is hardest. But you need a good healthy ego in this world to look out for yourself, I'll tell you that."

"Isn't it the truth," Liv said, linking her arm in his. "You're a man of real understanding."

"But you're confused, I think," the young woman timidly suggested. "You see, egotism is the sickness of an unhealthy ego. The holy man was referring to Liv's ego, not the grandchildren's."

"Surely not," said the jolly man, patting Liv's arm that had encircled his and smiling sweetly at her. "Tell me what he said."

Liv found that she did not want to repeat the holy man's words. He had hurt her feelings and now this nice man was repairing them. He was on her side.

Liv and he walked ahead on the trail, enjoying their rapport.

19

EXASPERATION

The other three women watched Liv and the jolly man go off together.

"I could kill her," one of them said, totally exasperated.

The other two laughed.

"How do you treat someone like a holy person when they're acting like a complete fool, when they just don't get it?" said the exasperated one.

"Maybe with Liv the message will seep in after a

while. She just hasn't really thought about it, and her new boyfriend is a bad influence."

"But if we're going to have trouble treating a nice woman like Liv as if she were holy, how will we do with mean people, with cheats and liars and racists?"

"Maybe people like that have never been treated kindly and courteously before. Maybe when we're nice, they'll be nice back."

"And if they're not, we just don't let it bother us because we have nothing riding on it. I think that's the secret, not to be invested in their behavior, not to get exasperated and want to kill them." She laughed again.

"It will be easy. What's hard about just being decent to everyone?"

"Liv got it for a minute there. Then she lost it. But it will come back."

"What do you do with a man like that friend of hers who just says what everyone wants to hear?" said the exasperated one.

"Tell him to shut up."

Laughter.

"No, the idea is not to judge him—or anybody. We

have to give up getting mad at people for how they think or act, give up having prejudices about right and wrong."

"We'll just be wimps, then, spineless, not standing up for anything or against anything."

"No. We will have peace of mind and the freedom of mind to see into the truth of things."

20

HEART

Joe sat in the kitchen watching Helena create lunch. This provided every bit as much pleasure as listening to Ho's cello, watching Daniel dance, talking to Maria, Ed, Henri, or Kim. Intuition in motion. Intelligence and discipline in motion. Every move from cupboards to chopping boards to range was efficient, graceful, present. And, at the end, something delicious to eat. Everyone was happy when it was Helena's day to cook.

She was an African-American who had established a chain of cheap nutritional restaurants in poor areas that were also cooking schools. Eat right and learn how to cook it. Her rival for customers was McDonald's and one day she said to Kim, the marathoner, "I'm chasing but I'm not gaining. Any advice?"

He replied, "Let them come back to you. Reel them in."

The kitchen windows were open to the rock-strewn yard, and the boulder birds were flitting back and forth bringing food to their young, who were nestled in the crevices of the largest stones. Kim was wrestling rocks from one spot to another, his way of increasing his upper-body strength. Joe was not clear whether Kim was building something, demolishing something, or whether he had anything in mind at all besides lifting, carrying, and placing.

Sometimes Kim whistled as he worked, joining the birds' twitterings. Often during the ostensible silence of their day, the monks were heard to autonomously whistle, sing, or laugh.

Suddenly Joe felt his heart flopping around in his chest like a big beached fish. He took a heart pill from his robe pocket and drank it down with some water, being sure this action was out of Helena's purview.

He wasn't certain he needed to take the pill at that moment. Maybe it was just for pain, not for his heart acting like a fish with a hook in its mouth.

I am getting dependent on my heart pills, he thought glumly.

He had not told the monks about his heart trouble since they were upset already about him spending the winter alone. As it was he'd had to promise to get a cellular phone in case he was in trouble, meaning dying. Joe imagined calling for help and their sending a helicopter. That would be the day. How embarrassing. How ignoble. He would never do it.

Helena, as if sensing his discomfort, some trouble in his mind or heart, came to the table and sat beside him on the bench. She put an arm around him, kissed his cheek.

Joe smiled.

All the monks were affectionate with him. Even the men gave him hugs and kisses.

Helena and Joe sat silently together.

When Daniel came into the kitchen and saw them sitting so close and so contentedly, he felt jealous. It seemed to him that Joe preferred the other monks to him, that he shared intimate moments with them and not with him. He felt like a snake was inside him, coiling around his innards, squeezing, filling his throat with bile. He poured himself a cup of tea and stood with his back to them.

Joe, with his powers of insight, understood what Daniel was feeling but realized that any gesture he made toward him would worsen the situation, that any acknowledgment would only embarrass him.

He knew that Daniel was troubled. He seemed to be feeling resentment, as well as jealousy. Joe considered resentment one of the worst of the evils, worse than envy or hate or egotism, although all the feelings were kin. But resentment was insidious; it ate up your vitals. It alienated you from your comrades. You felt wronged, a victim. And you wanted to get even.

Partly it was that Daniel was getting old for a dancer. The honed instrument, the kinetic sculpture that was his body, had begun to fail him and Daniel could no longer attain the standards set in his mind. He was famous but not as famous as he had hoped and now, clearly, he had reached the peak of his powers, and although these powers were more than adequate, they were not astonishing. All too soon they would not even be adequate.

Joe wished there was a pill for a snake that was feeding on the bitterness in Daniel like his heart pill that hopefully would calm the fluttering fish.

Helena returned to her cooking, Joe went to the window to observe Kim at his work and Daniel joined him there. Kim, with a big rock in his arms, unable to see where he was going, was staggering around in circles, tipping precariously to one side. He walked smack into one of the standing monoliths, rebounded off it, dropped the rock he was carrying, and sat down hard on the ground, looking extremely surprised. Joe and Daniel burst out laughing together, vaporizing the creatures inside them, which were released on the gust of their laughter.

21

SHIRKER

Among the monks there was a shirker. It was the poet, Ed. He showed up for chores late and left early. He always took the easiest job, grumbled while he worked, and did it in an unsatisfactory way so it often had to be redone by one of the others. When it was his turn to go to town for supplies, he never made the trip in one day but took two days, thereby missing two days of chores and having a night on the town as well.

Mostly he tried to get out of going to town.

One day it was his turn to go to town and he said he had a headache. He couldn't go. The headache also precluded his doing his chores. He was coming down with something.

That evening, when the monks met in the common room, they discussed Ed's headache, trying and failing to be charitable. All of them were dubious about his illness except for Helena, who believed him. "He is really quite miserable," she said. "He's sick as a dog."

They considered whether one of them should take his place going for supplies, but they were disinclined to do so. "Let's wait him out," said Henri. "We can just eat rice and beans until he gets well."

"If he's playing sick, why should we suffer?" said Daniel, the dancer. "Why not go down the hill and get the fruit and vegetables but not let the malingerer have any?"

"That's mean," said Helena. "If he's sick, he needs a proper diet. He needs vitamins."

"*If* is the key word," said Henri dryly.

"Let's ask Joe what to do."

They sought out the holy man, who was sitting in

his room, thinking. He did not always join them in the evening, sometimes choosing not to break his silence. The bedrooms were on the second floor, simply furnished with a single bed, a bureau, a bookshelf, a closet, a wooden chair.

Joe was sitting in his chair and it somehow seemed to the monks a beautiful sight. Sometimes when they had gone a day or even a few hours without seeing him, and came upon him unexpectedly (or, like now, expectedly), he took their breath away.

The holy man listened to the problem and told them he would talk to Ed.

He went to Ed's room and sat at the end of his bed, looking at the poet, who lay with his eyes closed but did not appear to be sleeping.

Ed opened one eye, saw Joe, and groaned. It was quite a good groan but not that good. In fact, Ed had the grace to blush at his groan, but it would take a sharp eye to detect the blush, a mother's eye, which Joe had.

Then Ed actually had the temerity to croak, "W-a-a-ter-r."

"This is a very sad case," Joe said. "A downed poet,

a poet unable to contribute to the community any longer, or live in harmony with us, a poet who in fact is causing a schism in the community, breaking it into a pro-Ed camp and an anti-Ed camp—the pro-Ed being a very small camp indeed, by the way."

Ed stirred uncomfortably and did not repeat his request for water.

"I am always careful to invite to my hermitage those persons I believe to have their feet upon the path, but it seems this time I have chosen a troublemaker whose feet are, most of the time, upon the bed. I shall have to ask you to go."

This was very shocking to Ed. It was very unlike the kindly holy man to be so firm, to be so, as it sounded to Ed in the weakened state he imagined himself to be, brutal. It scared him so much he began to shake, as if with the ague, and therefore to begin to believe himself truly sick.

"I can't go. I'm too sick. I think I am dying." He groaned a real groan and his body continued to shiver. Ed actually would rather die than be tossed out of the hermitage, where he had spent the happiest and most fruitful days of his life. What a fool he had been to let his native laziness jeopardize his stay here.

Joe, seeing the dramatic emotional reaction Ed was having to his words, said, "I have never claimed to be a healer, but I think I will try it right now. It's possible that I can heal. I wouldn't be at all surprised."

Joe stood up, took a deep breath, gazed at Ed, and said loudly, "Poet, stand up and be well."

As he spoke the words, he simultaneously grabbed hold of the poet, dragged him from the bed, and stood him on his feet, giving him something very like a box on the ears while he was at it.

"It worked," said the holy man happily. "I am a healer."

Ed had to laugh. "You're right. I'm healed."

"You look like a new man."

"I am," said Ed, still laughing. "I feel wonderful."

"It's amazing."

"Joe, I am so much better mentally, emotionally, and physically that I don't think you'll ever have trouble with me again. If you will please just give me one more chance."

"Of course I will," said the holy man. "In return I

must ask you to tell no one of these fabulous healing capabilities I've discovered. I would not want the world to think I can produce miracles."

However, the others, seeing Ed toiling so robustly, efficiently, and good-heartedly from then on, told each other it was one.

22

CHOICE

I have so many troubles, I don't know where to begin," said the man in his early forties, with a face unhappy enough to back up his claims.

"Nothing goes right for me in my life. I continually find I am in abusive relationships, first with my father, then my wife, and since my divorce, with other friends and lovers. I know that I must seek out the wrong people, but how do I stop? Even understanding my problems, and God knows I have had plenty of therapy, I keep ending up with the wrong people in my life. This is also true in my job situation. Even my children ill-treat me. Even my dog!"

The holy man listened as the man went on in this vein and then, during a pause, asked, "How do you feel about your height?"

"My height? I don't think about it." He frowned and puckered his lips. "Height?" he considered. "My height is all right. Why?"

"For those of us who are not born into an in-escapable prison of poverty and disease," said the holy man, "there is a world of choice open to us. I have reflected long upon this matter and now understand that the only thing we have no choice about in life is our height. That is the only thing that is a given. We get to complain about our height and that is all."

"That would be a silly thing to complain about," said the pilgrim from his lofty stance of having so many serious things to protest.

"Yes, very silly, since we can't do anything about it." Joe smiled. "But not so silly as complaining about all the troubles in our life we can choose to change."

PERSECUTED WOMAN

Joe talked to a middle-aged woman who was so impressive in her manner, character, and intelligence it was hard to believe she had a care in the world.

She had greeted him most graciously and now they were seated on the bench by the door where he was wont to talk to pilgrims when the occasion presented itself.

"In the town where I live, I have an enemy who is step by step destroying my life. And please, I beg of you, don't tell me to turn my other cheek. I tried that at first and she only proceeded to do me more and more harm."

Jesus' words leapt to the holy man's mind: *Whosoever shall smite thee on thy right cheek, turn to him the other also.*

"This woman has told terrible lies about me and as a result I have lost my job, my husband has divorced me, many of my friends have abandoned me."

"You do not look at all like a woman who has suffered such a nightmare," said Joe admiringly.

"Because I have had a chance to be away from the plague of her. I have healed among your pilgrims on this lovely mountain. But being away from home is not a solution. I will not be driven from my own town by this vermin, the town I have lived in all my life and love every inch of. Holy Man, I am not a perfect woman by a long shot. I have many flaws. But I swear that the stories she tells about me are lies. She has even taken me to court, sued me, and won!"

And if any man will sue thee at the court and take away thy coat, let him have thy cloak also.

Joe tried to imagine how he would feel if someone sued him for his two extra robes. Would he follow Christ's noble injunction? He hadn't done such a good job of giving up his robe to the famous man.

Love your enemies, bless them that curse you, pray for them which despitefully use you.

This certainly was Jesus' hardest command, thought Joe, but in any case this woman, right up front, has forbidden me to draw from his counsel regarding her persecution problem.

"Do you think she will kill you?" Joe asked.

"No, I do not. That is the one thing she won't do."

"That's great. Plato said of Anytus and Meletus, 'They can kill me, but they can't harm me.' He smiled and spread his hands as if her problem were solved.

"Holy Man. Forgive me, but she has already harmed me incredibly as I think you heard me tell you, although you did seem to be thinking of other things."

"But I see you as wonderfully unharmed! You are very well. You are free. You have discovered your true friends, have you not?"

"Well, yes, in a way I have."

"Your life is stripped to its essence, is pure gold. You are healthy, smart, and strong. How lucky you are."

"Oh, really? Tell me."

"I have just told you. Whereas this poor enemy of yours is either deluded in her mind about you or has been deceived by others in regard to you or is consumed by envy. Your enemy is not well or healthy or strong and is unable to think straight or see straight because of her obsession with you."

"Yes, but . . ."

"And so I urge you to be gentle in your thoughts about her. She doesn't know what she is doing. She can't help herself. She can't go on with her life as you can, as you have, as you are doing now, growing and learning. You will no longer let this poor, weak creature have the power to upset you."

"When you put it that way . . ."

"I see you as one who is already reconciled and from this position of strength you can easily be kind. Go forth and be so."

The woman smiled. "Yes, yes, I will. You have convinced me." She stood to go. Then she laughed and chided him, "Have you noticed that what it all comes down to is pretty much 'turning the other cheek'?"

"It does a little." Joe pondered. "Humm, yes, I see what you mean."

There's almost no improving on the words of the master, Joe thought.

24

FUSSINESS

It was Maria's day to cook. Joe watched her, feeling bemused. Unlike Helena who was always present, Maria's mind was not on it. She was thinking of other things, a science experiment, no doubt, moving distractedly from one chore to the other, burning herself once, leaving the faucet running twice, and three times bumping some part of her body, stifling exclamations.

Gradually the monks entered the kitchen and placed themselves at the long table, first taking bowls from the open shelves, or plates if they were having scrambled eggs and toast instead of cereal. When Henri, the lawyer, sat down, Joe realized that he always sat in the same place at the table. The others, consciously or otherwise, had learned to leave it available for him.

Humm, thought Joe.

Covertly he looked at Henri. He noticed the sleeves of his robe were each impeccably folded three times to leave his forearms free.

Humm.

Then he noticed that he wasn't taking any food, had not even selected a plate or bowl. Watching, Joe learned that Henri was waiting for the blue plate that Helena was using. When she was finished and had washed it, Henri went to get it for himself, then sat down again at his place, serving himself from the platter on the table, a portion of, by now, rather cold eggs.

Henri did not used to be so particular, Joe thought.

The next morning, Joe sat down in Henri's place. When Henri came in and saw Joe there, he flushed, feeling upset.

Joe was imperturbable and seemed to take no notice. The others did notice and were uneasy.

Henri stood irresolute, paced a little, then took his blue plate and sat down elsewhere.

That night, when they were free to talk, he went up to Joe and asked, "Why did you sit down at my place at the table this morning? I feel that it was intentional."

For an answer, Joe seized Henri's thrice-folded sleeve and pulled it down. He walked away.

"What is the matter with Joe?" Henri asked the others, feeling bewildered.

"He must think something is the matter with you," said Maria.

The next morning when Henri walked into the kitchen, Joe was standing there with the blue plate in his hands. He dropped it on the floor. It broke. Everyone was astonished. Joe got the broom and dustpan and cleaned it up.

That evening, Henri lay in wait for Joe and nabbed him when he came into the common room. "Okay, you think I have gotten too fussy about things, right?"

116

"Right," said Joe, pleased.

"But what is the matter with liking certain things and certain ways? I don't understand your aversion to

my behavior. Surely it is not harmful. Come on, Joe. Loosen up."

"You feel I have violated you, but I am setting you free. I am loosening *you* up. Particularity leads to peculiarity and then to pathological behavior. The three Ps. It is very insidious. You would eventually end up in a box. If you try to control your environment, it will soon control you. And everyone else around you will always have to be making adjustments to your maddening idiosyncracies."

"Maybe so, but I still don't think there's any harm in it."

"The most profound line in the Lord's Prayer is 'Lead us not into temptation but deliver us from evil.'"

"Evil?" Henri protested. "You're saying my behavior is evil?"

"We want to be free from desire, do we not?"

"Yes."

"Because it leads to temptation which leads to evil which is also slavery. If it weren't slavery, the words 'deliver us' would not be used."

"Okay, so?"

"You are beginning to enslave yourself with your fussiness. Therefore you are in evil."

"That is a very big stretch, Joe."

Joe smiled. "Yes, but I like it. I have shown you how to deliver yourself. Now you will be free to love, free to be good."

Henri shook his head.

"Let us take another tack. We deplore attachment, do we not?"

"Yes."

"Because attachment leads to suffering."

"Yes."

"You are attached to your place at the table and to the blue plate. I forbear thinking of other possible quirks, how you align your books on the shelf or which of your teeth are the first to be brushed, possibly the canines."

Henri shrugged ruefully. "I guess I see what you're saying."

Joe smiled. "Let me say in conclusion that developing and embracing these peculiarities will make you forget that you are enlightened, that you are a holy person."

"But I never knew that," he protested. "I never thought that."

"Yes you did, but you forgot. You must live your life in such a way that you will remember."

"And what happens when I remember? What do I do then?"

"Then you can forget about it."

25

DELUSION

There were two in the line who were as night and day, Jacob and Anna, and they both had secrets. Jacob's secret was eating him up, Anna's was sustaining her.

She was in her mid-thirties, from Scotland, a quiet, retiring woman whom everyone in the line was nevertheless drawn to because of her joyousness and peacefulness. They would crowd about her when the line broke for the day, wanting to talk to her or simply be with her. Also she was a nurse and amiable about tending any cuts or bruises, or listening to long sad stories of aches and pains, past illnesses and present. She herself rarely spoke, which made it more amazing that she had such an effect on them all.

Strange to say, sad or perhaps happy to say, some of the pilgrims, after spending time with Anna, no longer felt it necessary to wait and see the holy man and so started home with buoyant step.

Many wondered about her, unable to understand what someone so happy in herself was doing here in the line but, when asked why she needed to see the holy man, she said nothing. This was her secret.

Jacob had the opposite effect on the pilgrims. They did not shun him exactly, but there was something so dark, so almost dangerous-seeming about him, that they kept their distance. He was a large, muscular man in middle age, a European with a chiselled, bony, clenched face that looked like it might fall off if he tried to smile.

He did not care that they kept apart from him. His job was to see the holy man, tell him his secret, and that was it. If relief came with the telling of it, maybe he would take on life again. If not, he would put an end to himself. Over and out.

Anna was not far ahead of him in the line, and he

was aware of her popularity. He was interested that this small, quiet, unglamorous woman could generate such enthusiasm, but he was not jealous. He had never cared whether people liked him or not. Geniality was not his strong suit. They admired and respected him. Some possibly feared him. He had a few genuinely close friends and there were women who had passionately loved him—for a time.

If anything, he thought, this Anna is happy because she is a fool. She knows nothing of the dark underbelly of life where the maggots are.

But it was hard to maintain this fiction after spending two minutes with the woman—or the one second it took to feel her glance looking straight into his heart and not shrinking from what she saw there, not forgiving him but, as he saw it, allowing him.

As the days passed, he found himself observing her more and more closely, subsequently wanting to be near her and, when he was near her, feeling willing to make himself attractive to her.

He began to think that if he had such a woman in his life, someone so good as Anna loving him, then everything would be all right. It was that simple. His depression, which seemed unconquerable, could be abated in a minute if he could have her for his own, like drinking a magic potion.

When he would come home at night, her face would light up to see him and his heart would fill with gladness. All this black despair that weighed him down would be cast away.

He had the insight to ask himself why a face already so alight would light up to see such a one as he, but he brushed the question aside.

And when he asked himself why such a treasure would love a brute like himself, he answered that he was a partly good brute—he had shared his wealth with the needy, had helped young men on in their careers, been a loving father to his sons despite the toll of his divorces. Anna would bring out the good that was in him.

Already he felt better imagining their life together. And it wouldn't be one-way. In return for her love and peace and boundless good humor he would do many nice things for her: reward her with clothes, jewels, travels, and houses in different lands—all the things women so loved. And since she was younger and would want children, he would be happy to provide.

So Jacob lived in his fantasy and was seen almost to smile successfully and be charming on occasion and the pilgrims felt a little bit more comfortable around him.

Until the night he joined Anna's circle, carrying sticks he had gone far afield to gather for her fire, and he heard her speak of her husband and children.

It was not the flaring fire that caused the red-hot heat to charge to his face but a mixture of rage and shame.

He turned abruptly and disappeared into the surrounding darkness. What right had she to be in this line alone for all this long time, portraying herself as a single, available woman? She had lured him on, given him hope, been profligate with her smiles and warm gestures, wooed him with her gentle ways. When she looked at him, he'd felt so alive, so important, as if he had a right, after all, to be on this earth. He believed she cared for him. But she hadn't. She'd made a fool of him, deluded him. Now he hated himself more.

When he cooled down he admitted to himself that he, not she, had been the deluder. And she did care for him—exactly as much as she cared for the others. The real delusion had been his belief in an instant magic-potion cure, the idea that someone else could make him better.

The holy man wouldn't make him better either. He was lost.

"Are you all right?" He felt the balm of her presence next to him. He could not remember anyone ever asking him if he was all right.

"No," he sighed, a new sound for him.

"Tomorrow we will see the holy man," she said.

"It won't help."

"Maybe not. But you'll see him. And then . . . who knows?"

He felt a wave of utter hopelessness.

At the same time, in the darkness, he felt the muscles of his face unclench, his lips fall apart, his brow clear. His face, letting go in this way, allowed the lines of age and sorrow to reveal themselves on the infinitely tired flesh.

Anna was peering up at him. "At least now," she said, "you are ready."

26

THE ONE

Every time Joe opened the door to a pilgrim, with his eyes full of welcome, a smile on his lips, he was hoping it would be the one he was waiting for. Not the one or two or three who might spend the winter with him, but the one to whom he hoped to pass on his teachings, who would take his place when he died, spreading the word of the inherent holiness of people and nature, the need for kindliness and learning.

Many wonderful people had come his way. Many had become monks and part of his community. But none of them was the person he had in his mind. He never doubted he or she would come. But now many years had gone by without the appearance of such a one, and he felt that his days were winding down. He or she had better hurry.

He opened the door and there she stood, a woman in her middle thirties, with short, straight, red hair, brown eyes, an air of absolute balance and possession, a look that was at once grave and happy.

Joe and Anna fell into each other's arms like long-lost friends and for a confused minute, Joe thought, no, this isn't the one, it is my dearest daughter returned to me, for when Joe was a young man, both his wife and his daughter were killed in a terrible accident. He had to give them back.

"I have been looking all over for you," Anna said.

"I have been waiting for you," said Joe.

They talked together for an hour. Mostly Joe listened. It emerged she had been dreaming about him for years. The face in the dream was clearly his, now that she saw him. But, as there was no picture of Joe anywhere in the world, there was nothing she could match her dream face to. She looked. She went to see the different holy men who came to her country and she read all she could about the ones who existed in remote parts of the world.

When she began to hear about him, she felt he was the one, but it was so hard for her to get away. She had a job as a nurse, was married, and had a small child. She began to save her vacation time and her money, but then she had another child and, later, was put in charge of the clinic where she worked. Nevertheless she continued to make her plans. Finally the day came when she'd arranged care for the children, a replacement at work, and could commence her journey—her husband, friends, and colleagues all thinking her quite mad and rather angry with her, to tell the truth.

"But now it has taken so long to get to your door that I am overdue home. I was hoping I might stay for a while, but it is impossible. I'm sorry."

"I am sorry too." It was a huge understatement. Joe's heart sank in his chest, seemed to retreat to the far corners of the waters of his body, barely afloat.

"But I'm so glad I came. My experience in the line, among the pilgrims, was unforgettable. And then to meet you at last, spend this hour with you, is like being reuinted with an identical twin. I feel so moved by our connection."

Joe told her about his work, about the hermitage life. He said he tried to teach people to honor each other, strive toward excellence in one's own life no matter how insignificant one's work, live fully, fearlessly, dedicated to learning and kindliness, enemies of anger and greed. He said, "You are welcome to stay as long as you can, but I understand your predicament . . ."

Joe faltered. He didn't understand. Why had she been given to him at last, only to be snatched away?

She gazed deeply at him and asked, "What do you think it meant, my having this ongoing dream of you? Isn't it strange? I know you don't need me in any way but, well, can I do anything for you before I go? Are you feeling all right? I am a nurse, after all."

Joe was overcome. He found that he could not tell her who she was and what she meant to him.

"I am feeling fine, Anna. I understand the calls of your family and job. I am not sure what the dreams mean. It is wonderful that you surmounted such difficulties to come all this way. I am profoundly happy to know that you are here . . . in the world."

When they parted, they embraced again and Anna wept. "I have to confess that I don't want to go," she said. "I don't want to leave you. I feel I am making a big mistake. But . . . I am so torn!"

Again Joe had it on the tip of his tongue to outright ask her to stay, or else at least to go home and consider a return, go home and settle her affairs for a final return so that he might pass down the mantle of his wisdom— but the words balked, refused to leap from his tongue to the air between them. He did not want to seem to beseech her. He felt the decision must be entirely hers. And deep in his heart he also felt that the work she was doing was perhaps more important than being with him.

And so Anna went away. He watched until she was out of sight, the one he'd waited for all these years. He felt a sob rise up in his breast and he let it come, let the tears come, and for a few minutes, all his wisdom could not help him deal with this mighty disappointment.

Then he recovered and remembered his own words, that he was happy she was here in the world. She would find her way without him. Even if she didn't get to teach thousands, as he had, still, every person who passed through her life would be touched by her holiness and there would be a ripple effect.

I could have asked her to stay, Joe thought. Jesus called his apostles away, saying, "Follow me," and that was that, they dropped everything—family, work, everything, and came. Gautama Buddha left his spouse and children. So why couldn't I ask Anna to do so? Well, I couldn't. I am me, not Them. It didn't feel right. It would have been bad action.

27

KILLER

After seeing Anna off, Joe felt he could not go on receiving that day—he would do better to close up shop. However, after spending an hour alone, he recovered his balance and decided to press on. The season was almost over and there were still so many in the line.

He had about a dozen run-throughs and then Jacob came to the door, greeted him as the holy man, and introduced himself. Joe invited him to sit down and tell his story.

His words came with difficulty, punctuated by deep sighs.

"When I was a teenager, I left home and set out to wander the world, taking odd jobs as I went. I was curious about other countries."

Joe too had spent years of wandering, but he had been older than Jacob when he set out, in his thirties, and he was not so much curious as lost and despairing.

"One night, when I was seventeen years old, I found myself in a French port, in a bar, having a wild time with some other young fellows, and it struck me that traveling wasn't enough—I needed a far grander experience, something with danger and drama. And so, I joined the French Foreign Legion for a period of four years.

"I determined to be a first-rate soldier, one of the elite. I was sent to Vietnam. This was before America entered the war. I fought the Vietcong and the Red Kyhmer. I was trained by a superb officer—how to move quietly through the jungle, how to kill quietly with a knife or bare hands my worthy opponents. I was very good. This went on for three years. I became a lieutenant. Remarkably, I wasn't seriously injured, a few knife wounds.

"Then the Legion decided to pull me out and send me to Algeria. When I and my men were leaving the plane and heading for the terminal, I was shot in the back. I was sent to a hospital in Paris and told I didn't need to serve my last year. I stayed around Paris until my wound healed completely and then I went home.

"Everyone at home thought I had been traveling the world. I didn't want them to know the truth. I was no longer the boy who'd gone off in search of excitement, although I thought myself a fine, brave fellow. The only person I told was my mother, and she said she didn't want a killer in her home. This was very deflating, but it was true. Maybe if I had been defending my own country, it would have been different. But I was a mercenary. I and some of my buddies had already been approached by different foreign powers for the high-paying job of assassin.

"I put that period of my life out of my mind as if it never existed. I was only twenty. I went back to school, got a business degree, and opened a store—a very tame life. The shop did well, became a chain of stores, and I was rich. I married and had three boys."

"Did you tell your wife and children?" Joe asked.

"No. I had taken my mother's reaction to heart. I couldn't ask a wife to understand the cruelty and bestiality I engaged in. Even if you have been to war, you can't. Maybe there is nothing to understand because it is so senseless.

"And my boys? They would have admired me more, like a movie star action hero. I could not abide that.

"I have had a good life, worked hard, and been a lucky man. I have not suffered the bad reactions and the nightmares one hears can happen to veterans. I have always been careful not to get into fights for fear I would unthinkingly use my skills and kill somebody. I have lived as a peaceable person, trying to do the right thing—until recent years when I have become unapproachable because of my gloominess. My wife left me. Other wives left me. I don't blame them. I have a hatred for life.

"I keep thinking about those boys I killed, and how they didn't get to live a life, any kind of life, good or bad. I took their lives from them. I can't forgive myself for this. I find I am thinking about it almost constantly. I can see their faces which, because of me, are not always attached to their bodies. Crying heads.

"And so, I heard about you and thought maybe it would help to tell you about it. People say that confession is good for the soul. But I can already tell it hasn't helped. I'm not afraid to die. Death is just over and out. I think that is the answer."

"Life is suffering," Joe said. "You have heard of the penitents who, in the old days, carried huge wooden crosses on their backs to express contrition for their sins. You are carrying a very heavy cross, only it is in your head and heart."

Joe took one of Jacob's hands in his. "I think you were wise to put your warrior years behind you, not to continue with violence or let your memories drag you down into the mire. You have lived a decent life and it is because you are a good man that you are thinking these thoughts that fill you with sorrow. Jacob, I believe that we can create ourselves anew each day, and you have had thirty years to do so! You are not a killer anymore. But if you take your life you will die a killer. Your last breath will be the breath of a killer."

Jacob released his hand to brush tears from his eyes.

"I know . . . but I can't take it any more." He said good-bye abruptly and went away.

The holy man found the cellist, Ho, and pulled him from his chores. "Follow that man down the mountain and stay with him. If he goes to a bar, drink with him. If he tries to kill himself, protect him. He is scared because he has just let his demons out of their box, but I think if he can survive this night, he will begin to be better.

"Ho, imagine a man who fought three years in Vietnam, leaving a toll of uncountable dead, and has never spoken a word about it to anyone until today. He is from a country that has no Vietnam veterans. His shame and guilt are unendurable, but worst of all is his loneliness."

The cellist was a veteran of a war in China. It didn't matter that it wasn't Vietnam. All wars are the same and wreak the same excruciating sorrow. Ho had come to Joe with the same feelings as the man who had just left. There were men all over the world with these feelings. So had it always been. So would it always be until there was an end to ignorance, anger, and greed and men treated each other with honor as they would treat a holy man.

28

THE PUZZLE

Ho found Jacob sitting on the fence, watching the dappled ponies. He introduced himself and climbed upon the top rail next to the legionnaire, who sat with one hand, palm up, nestled in the other, an unconscious lotus position.

Jacob's face that had released itself into lines last night was now worn into grooves from the tears he had shed with the holy man. "These are marvelous beasts," he said.

They watched together for a while and, even though the cellist had not spoken, Jacob said defensively, "There is nothing to say, you know. My mind is made up. I have only stopped for a minute on my way to the grave, to observe this baffling game."

"It is up to you," Ho said. "I understand. I was a veteran too. So was Joe. Not long after he returned from his war, which was the second world war, as if he hadn't seen enough of blood and death, his wife and child were killed in a car accident. He was in his twenties then . . ."

Ho told Jacob about Joe's life and Jacob listened with a keen interest. Periodically the ponies galloped past them or scrambled together in front of them as their riders competed for the ball. He told about Joe's suffering, his wandering, searching, studying, learning from different sages, finally coming to this mountain to build his hermitage. Ho spoke of all the people who had, like himself, come to live with Joe and learn from him, but how Joe always sent them back out into the world to enrich it.

"Now he is old and some of us are afraid he is not very well. The time has come for him to choose some- one to take his place. He has been waiting for many years for a special person he said was coming, but I guess he has given up. We thought he might have especially called us together this summer to choose one of us. There is one monk who ardently wishes to be chosen."

"I hope he will not choose that one," said Jacob, drawn into the problem, his mind struggling free from himself.

Ho held on to the railing with one hand and gestured with the other as he talked. Jacob still sat balanced with one hand within the other as if nursing it, protecting it.

"Today there is a rumor floating around among us that Joe found someone from the line who is the one he has been waiting for, but that he lost the person. So now, Jacob, I have to humbly admit my real purpose in following you is to ask if you came to know anyone in the line who was remarkable."

"Yes." The heavy features of the legionnaire lifted into a smile. "Anna, of course. Anyone will tell you. She is very uncommon."

Ho nodded.

"Why didn't the holy man ask her to stay?"

"Well, he certainly wanted to, but Joe is humble,

you know, and I think it seemed to him that what she was doing in the world was more important than sharing the last days of an old man like him." Ho, surprisingly, laughed.

Jacob frowned. "It is not funny. It seems like a terrible misunderstanding. I don't think either Anna or Joe would like to hear you laugh." Jacob's eyes were afire now, and he locked the monk in his gaze. "Maybe you are the man who is so eager to be chosen," he challenged.

"Maybe I am," said Ho as if to deliberately provoke the old warrior. "Who wouldn't want to take the place of the holy man and have the whole world come to sit at his feet? He laughed again. "Not that Joe lets anyone sit at his feet."

Again Jacob was offended by the monk's laugh. "A monk should not be ambitious. Joe would not want such a one to take his place," said Jacob.

"Quite right." Ho shrugged. "But this Anna, in her goodness, harbored no such desire and therefore went away. What is one to do?"

"It is a puzzle," Jacob said.

Ho climbed down from the fence. "I must go on to

the town for supplies. I hope you will be all right. What is the matter with your hand?"

"This?" Jacob looked at the hand he'd been harboring. "Well, you see, the holy man held this hand in his own. So now I am thinking, how can I possibly turn it against myself, this blessed hand? Instead I must put it to some good work." He paused to cough and wave away the dust cloud stirred up by the skirmishing ponies. "I have an idea what I could do."

THE GAME

That night in the common room, Ho told the holy man, "Your legionnaire, Jacob, stopped to watch the game and was so entranced he forgot for a time that he was hell-bent on putting an end to himself."

"What about when he remembers? Such anguish as he feels will be uppermost in his mind."

"We had a long talk and I gave him something else to think about. I spurred him to action. Unlike our stumpy-legged ponies, old warriors need to be spurred."

"Yes and meanwhile the game is an excellent distraction. It's funny how you forget about it, except when you're there, and then you can hardly tear yourself away."

"What game?" asked the others. "Game?"

"The one with the ponies."

"The dappled ponies down there in the pasture?"

"Yes," said Ho. "It's sort of like polo. You ride the ponies and hit a ball toward a goal with a mallet if the ball hasn't already got away from you by rolling away downhill in the opposite direction." Ho laughed.

"I've been up and down that trail a hundred times," said Helena, "and I've never seen this game you're speaking of."

"Nor have I," the others backed her up.

"Have you seen the ponies running up and down and doing their twists and turns and fancy steps?" Ho asked.

"Yes."

"Well, not everyone sees the riders," Ho said.

"Come on."

"It's true. The riders are ghosts. I think they are ghosts of old warriors because it seems that only those who have been to war can see them."

"You mean only veterans are cracked enough to think they see them," Helena said. Everyone laughed.

Ho and the holy man wandered outside. "The stars look so close you could run your fingers through them," Ho said. "But where is the moon?"

"It's in the spring," said Joe, pointing to the liquid circle at the foot of the biggest boulder where the moon floated, trembling in the slight breeze.

After a little silence, Ho said, "Remember you told me how you completely lost your reason over that game? You were so fascinated by it you just about gave up being a holy man and spent all your time down there watching."

"Yes. Along with everything else about it, it seemed to be a parable for life. Going forwards and backwards and round in circles, striving ever forward only to have to run like crazy backwards to get the ball again, realizing that your enemy is after the same goal and you're actually helping him toward it and getting roughed up and possibly killed while you're at it but still feeling the comradeship of being in the game all together."

Joe laughed and shook his head.

"Naturally I figured that if I could only understand the game, I would understand the meaning of life."

"And . . ."

"Well, I came to realize that I had better go back to the hermitage to eat and sleep and do my chores or I was going to die sitting there on that fence and before that I was going to go crazy."

Ho laughed. "Like Buddha under the Bodhi tree, sitting and fasting, realizing he wasn't going to reach samsara if he didn't get something to eat."

Joe smiled.

Ho drew a big breath and asked the holy man what he thought of his theory the others had laughed at. "Joe, do you think the riders are ghosts of dead warriors? Or maybe . . . could it be that we survivors are the ghosts?"

"You, a ghost, Ho? What a joke. You are not only alive, you are awake."

30

HAPPINESS

Kim left the enthusiastic young runners of the town who had been accompanying him thus far and started up the Hermitage Trail, moving fast and efficiently, breathing calmly, monitoring himself so as not to get into oxygen debt as he fought gravity to the top. His sure feet knew the trail so well, every rock and root, twist and slant, that he felt he could close his eyes. But he didn't. Every path, no matter how well known, contains the unexpected.

Kim was, as always, utterly happy while running, in accord with nature, in harmony with the universe, in touch with the truth that was in him, full of love for all creatures even to the lowliest insect. Sometimes Kim thought that if he weren't blessed with this gift of running he would not be a good monk, would not even be a good person. It somehow made him feel he was cheating. He would talk to Joe about it if he could find the words.

He was Korean: small, lithe, intricately muscular. His dark eyes danced with light. His hair, even cut close to his skull, had the black iridescence of a starling's wing, and his teeth were almost blindingly white. Everything about him seemed tuned to a higher degree than other mortals.

He reached the hermitage in one of his best times and, as always, his heart sang to see the sturdy white house sitting amidst the tumbled boulders.

After rinsing himself off in the makeshift outdoor shower, Kim searched out Joe.

It was evening now and Joe sat alone in the backyard with a volume of poetry in his lap but looking outward as if he were taking the words in through his thighs. He probably knows the poems by heart anyway, thought Kim.

Joe looked his way, smiled fondly, and patted the place next to him.

Kim sat down beside him on the rock, a long one Kim had tipped over to make a bench. The liquid sound of Ho's cello wafted faintly from the common room window, as if the farflung stars were sending a message.

"What's on your mind?" Joe asked.

Kim was quiet, then spoke slowly. "When I am running, I attain that no-mind that we all seek, that perfect emptiness, the one-ness. I'm not alone in that. It is nothing special, I guess, for anyone who works with devotion. I have talked with other athletes about it, artists too. But, Joe, given this happiness as a part of my daily life, it seems easy for me to be loving and kind. Is this true?"

"I think it is easier for the happy person to be kind. But also it follows that a kind person is a happy person."

"I feel like it is too easy for me."

Joe laughed. "Look what you have gone through to be the athlete you are. Incredible discipline. Unbearable loneliness. Denying yourself the food, drinks, festivities other young people enjoy. Enduring hours of tortuous training every single day, all the while understanding you must be willing, when the time comes, to undergo the anguish of losing the race, always understanding that one day you might hurt yourself and fall out of the race forever and, finally, accepting that, inescapably, you will grow old and slow. No, Kim, it is not so easy for you."

"It feels easy."

"Because you are a Buddha," said Joe.

"Can I stay here with you, Joe?"

Joe knew that he meant forever. "No, Kim. Not yet. It is good for you to be out in the world."

"You always tell us that."

"Because it is true, particularly for you. Many more people see you than see me, as you run marathons through the great capitals of the world. They get to see up close what a holy man looks like and behaves like because millions watching television see the grace and humility with which you accept the laurel wreath and listen carefully to the worthy words that you say. You are an inspiration. I have heard that you never reply to the reporters' questions but that, in the happiness of the moment, pure poetry flies from your tongue. Now, apparently, they don't even ask you about the race, just wait to hear what you have to say about anything. I wouldn't deprive the world of you, Kim."

"Isn't this hermitage the world? Isn't this boulder the world?"

"Yes, this boulder is the world, Kim. But there's no TV."

31

COVETOUSNESS

Daniel, the dancer, was born in South America and was part Indian, part Spanish. As a young, high-spirited youth, he had come with friends, on a lark, to the hermitage but then, moved by Joe's message, had stayed for a year. As time passed and he became a star, he returned often to the hermitage but gradually wandered off the path Joe had set him upon. However, he was gifted in hiding his fall from grace from others.

Now he stood at Joe's door with his uncannily perfect posture, his still beautiful face. Joe bid him enter and he sat on the one chair, while Joe sat on the end of the bed, his hands on his knees. He told Joe he wanted to stay.

Most of the other monks had come individually or together to tell Joe they wanted to spend the winter with him and now Daniel had come to do so.

"I must tell you as I've told the others that it is my winter to be alone," Joe said mildly.

"Maybe you are not considering the dangers. I think I should be with you."

"What about your dancing, Daniel?"

"I am finished. I am too old now. Because you urged all of us to give most of our money away, I cannot return to my country a man of substance. I will not be respected if I don't have a fine house, a really big house. That matters in my country." He laughed. "In any country. Sad but true. So, I want to remain here with you."

"Who are these people whose respect you so badly want?" asked Joe wonderingly.

"Just people. The man on the street. The men in the other fine houses. Women. I know it isn't right to feel that but I do."

"What about your friends? Isn't their respect more

important than these anonymous hordes? I thought you didn't want to retire. You were going to teach. You're only forty."

"I'm old and I'm sore and I'm tired."

"Those feelings will pass. Ask yourself which is the better of these two pictures ten years from now: The first picture is you in a fine house in any country of your choice, entertaining people you don't care about, eating and drinking too much, getting further into debt, divorced from the dancer's art and the music you love.

"The second picture is of you at fifty, passing on your knowledge to the young dancers who adore you and urge you every night to take supper with them, who come to you with their personal problems as well as their hopes and fears.

"Your apartment is small, but sitting in its chairs are people who want to be with you, Daniel, not strangers to make merry at your expense. And among your students is one boy or girl who you can already tell will be as great a dancer as you were, greater than you, so that when you are sixty and seventy you can say to yourself with satisfaction and pleasure, I was his teacher.

"And the young dancers will talk amongst themselves and ask each other, 'If Daniel was so famous, he must have made piles of money. Why does he live so simply and work so hard for us all?' And some old-timer will answer, 'Don't you know he gave all his money to create scholarships for poor dancers?' 'Really!' they'll exclaim, 'that's fantastic.'"

Joe sighed. This was the most talking he had done since the woman who was so scared to die had come. The holy chatterbox strikes again, he thought.

"You are always telling us to go back into the world and do our work. I feel it is a finer thing to stay here and live as you do, to give it all up completely."

Daniel didn't say that he didn't want to teach, that he really didn't like the young dancers, nor they him, although they admired him, or had until recently when he began to fail and lose the luster of fame, take on the hated taint of a has-been. And he had not created the scholarships Joe had referred to, although at one time he'd honestly meant to. Instead he'd made bad investments, throwing good money after bad, always thinking the scholarships could wait until he recouped his losses.

But now he saw how he could still be a star for the rest of his life if he could be chosen as Joe's successor.

Joe was at the end of his life. The one he had waited for had not come or, if the rumors were true, had come and then gone. Daniel believed Joe had asked his seven favorites there for the summer to choose from among them. And he felt he was the best choice. If nothing else, he looked the part, had a breathtaking, charismatic presence that Joe, in truth, sage though he was, didn't have at all.

Yet Joe, knowing what Daniel was asking, was silent.

"If you don't want me here," Daniel said humbly, "I will stay in the town for the winter. You will be able to call me if you need me. I will return to the hermitage in the spring to see that you are all right."

Because there were no pictures of the holy man in the world, because Joe and the monks all dressed alike and all equitably took their turns at going for supplies, indistinguishable from each other, Daniel presumed the townspeople thought the holy man remained always in his mountain aerie, ever unseen by any of them.

Also, because most of the pilgrims were rushed through the house with head-spinning speed, Daniel believed that few in the world would question the identity of the holy man if it were changed.

It briefly occurred to Daniel, flickered through his mind, that if Joe did not survive the winter, he could be on hand to discover the event and simply take his place as the holy man with no one the wiser.

He was scared by the audacity of the thought and then, when Joe's eyes rested on his, Daniel felt more scared that Joe was reading his mind. His heart accelerated, and he flushed. Quickly he lowered his eyes as he stood to go.

"I know all the townspeople," Joe said, almost aimlessly, looking idly out the window. "I played with them all as children. You would enjoy a winter in town but no, you must go back to your work."

"You are right of course," Daniel hastily agreed, feeling he'd had a narrow escape from evil or, worse, from its discovery . . . if indeed he had escaped.

Now Joe looked directly at Daniel, saying, "We are born, we suffer, we die. However, love is a possibility for us all and, for some few, there is also a big house."

Daniel could not resist asking, because he really wanted to know. "Need they be mutually exclusive? Can't we have both love and house?"

Joe smiled. "Certainly. But one must consider carefully how one goes about getting the house."

32

DANDELIONS

On one of the last evenings in the common room, Maria came up with the interesting news that early in the summer she and Helena had discovered a meadow full of dandelions, picked many bagfuls and, combining their knowledge of science and cuisine, had ventured to make a vat of dandelion wine which they subsequently bottled.

"Since we're soon parting and who knows when we'll all be together again," they said, "maybe we should broach a few bottles and see how it tastes."

Everyone seemed to think there was nothing wrong with that idea. Some of them were feeling quite down in the dumps at the idea of leaving Joe. So they were willing to taste the experiment. In no time at all, bottles were loosed from their racks, corks were popped, glasses filled.

The wine was a shimmering amber hue and it slipped down their throats like liquid sunshine. The lighthearted concoction seemed to have no effect at first but only because the kick was slow to arrive. It was a no-nonsense kick when it came. One minute they were decorously sitting about, idly, even gloomily, chatting, and the next they were up and dancing, telling stories, doing stunts, laughing their heads off, reciting poems, and seeing who could make the funniest face.

Joe appeared at the door, drawn by the noise. "Ah, you are trying out the dendelion wine. What a good idea. Any left for me?"

There was. They all made merry through the evening, forgetting dinner entirely, and when it was time for bed nobody went but instead slumbered together in a big wheat-colored pile, dreaming bright-yellow, soft-petaled dreams.

33

RICE RUN

There were only a few days left in which the holy man would be receiving the pilgrims. The nights had already turned cold and this morning a brief, dry snow had fallen, flakes that were no more than specks of glitter drifting lazily from the sky.

In the Woods of Clattering Leaves the gingko trees had turned yellow and soft so that the perpetual clattering ceased, replaced by a whispering sound of "time to leave, time to die," until one after another, they floated to the forest floor.

The hay was in for the stumpy-legged ponies, who

would soon be stabled for the winter. The boulder birds had flown away south.

The last cord of wood had been chopped and split for the hermitage stove. Joe needed six cords to see him through.

One by one, the monks were readying themselves to go and all (except for Ho, who kept maddeningly saying Joe would be fine) were still offering to stay, or urging Joe to winter in the town.

"No," he said, "you must return to your individual work, with renewed creativity and passion. And I must stay here in my home. There are too many distractions in the town. Winter is my most fruitful season for thinking. Maybe it is time to write down some of my thoughts."

"You always said you didn't believe in writing them down, that they got altered by trying to pin them down, that you had to pass on your teachings in person."

"I am not so inflexible that I can't change my mind about things."

"That's another reason why you didn't write them down because, you said, once the words were printed, you couldn't change your mind."

"Oh, go away. You are all getting so argumentative about everything, I will be glad to be rid of you. That is the trouble with intimacy, you have lost your awe of me and treat me like a child."

"I know," said Kim. "Instead of worshipping you, we love you."

They were going, one by one.

"Today, I will do the rice run," Joe said. "I will need twenty pounds."

They all wanted to do the rice run with him and help him carry the twenty-pound bag up the steep trail but, as usual, he refused to be accompanied and they didn't argue with him about this one thing because they knew that the rice run was sacrosanct.

Usually, when Joe went to town, the pilgrims were told that he wouldn't be receiving that day so that they needn't stand in line needlessly. But this day they were not told and so formed their line as usual.

"It is almost winter," they said to each other nervously. "How many more days will he see us?" Some of them, at the sign of that first light, dry, glittery snow, were getting ready to start back down.

Joe hiked to town and right to the park to play with

the children. "This is my last visit until the spring," he told them. "But you will see me at the first thaw. I love the winter time except for not seeing you children. I learn so much from you all. You are all so good."

Whereupon the children all told stories on each other about how bad they were. One beat up on his little sister. One didn't do what his mother said and talked smart to her. Another kept skipping school. Another stole candy from the store. On and on.

"You are all good as gold," Joe told them. "I love you with all my heart."

"We love you too, Joe," they said. "We wish it didn't have to be winter."

"Nothing lasts. Everything changes. But the changes are the same. Winter will always turn to spring."

"Will you always come down at the first thaw like you have every year?"

"As long as I can still put one foot in front of the other."

"If you can't we'll come up to see you."

"What a good idea!"

Joe bid them all goodbye, then struggled up the path with the twenty-pound bag of rice, making frequent stops, not because he needed to so much but because he enjoyed prolonging his last trip.

At one point, as he took a shortcut across an open field, wild chrysanthemums grew up in his footsteps.

The last half mile was the steepest and that was where the line began.

He set down the rice. "My goodness, that's heavy. "I'm not as strong as I used to be," he said to the man at the end.

"I can't leave my place in line or I'd help you. But, I tell you what. We'll pass the bag along the line and you can walk beside it."

"What a good idea!" said Joe as he had to the children.

And so they passed the bag of rice along, hands to hands, and Joe walked along, greeting everyone, smiling upon them, touching them, and saying, "This is so kind of you, to help out an old man. If you will treat everyone you meet with such helpfulness and kindness, you will be a happy person."

And so, as he passed them by, it came to them one by one that he was the holy man. They had gotten to see the holy man after all, those who had despaired to ever reach his door before the snows came, and he had spoken to them and touched them.

This was how Joe said goodbye to his last pilgrims every year so that no one went away disappointed, and it was called the rice run.

34

JOY

The pilgrims were gone. The trail began to heal and in the hermitage, Joe healed too.

The second floor was closed off for the winter and Joe made his home in the kitchen, with the wood-burning stove. He pushed the long table against the wall and, having brought down his mattress from the bedroom, put it on top. He brought a table and straight-back chair from the common room and a comfortable armchair. The winter outhouse, built high for the snow, wasn't far from the kitchen door and Joe had snowshoes.

He was mortally tired. It had been a long summer

and seeing hundreds of people almost every day had taken it out of him, more so than in previous years, maybe because of his heart. He was happy to be alone and to replenish himself.

But many years had passed since he'd been totally alone. He was in his twenties when he gave back his wife and daughter and that was when he dropped out of the life he'd known. Then he began to roam the world in search of meaning. He was solitary until, in Cambodia, he found the right teacher and stayed with him for almost ten years before coming here to build the hermitage, when it was the size of what was now the kitchen. Truly a hermit, he lived alone for some years until people began to seek him out.

He'd been here twenty-five years. It was hard to believe. He felt he had accomplished something in that time. He hoped so.

The winter weeks went by, then a month, then two. Joe began to feel a little lonely and useless. He was a teacher to the bone. It was hard to have no one to teach. He slept a lot and dreamed dreams. Sometimes he wondered if his waking moments were the dream, if it was summer really, and he was only dreaming that he was alone in the hermitage, surrounded by impenetrable snow.

He would ask himself why he was alone and he remembered that he wouldn't let any of the monks stay with him. Nor had he chosen any pilgrims from the line.

Then his mind would touch like a feather, oh so fleetingly, on the one who had come and gone.

Always Joe had carried his part of the hermitage load, taking his turn to cook, to sweep, or wash up, taking his turn to go to town for supplies, but the truth was the monks looked after him more than he realized and cooking every day was different from cooking once a week. Rice, beans, or bread took nearly an hour to cook and often, lost in his thoughts, he'd burn them. There were days when he contented himself with cups of tea or broth.

So it was that no sooner had he rested and restored his strength from the rigors of the summer than he began to lose strength for lack of food and to grow lightheaded, not realizing he wasn't eating enough.

One day he set his heart pills down on the counter, later absent-mindedly moved a jar in front of them, and never saw them again.

Living alone, the carved-in-stone schedule of the hermitage was no longer in existence and he often didn't know where in the day he was. Was it meditation time, or the hours for chores? Time to sleep, or had he just got up? Silent time presented no scheduling problems—that was constant.

The snow, drifting high against the kitchen windows, added to his disorientation.

He realized he must take himself in hand, care for himself, put order in his day, pay attention. He did so and his mind became clear as a running stream.

But then the roof of the storeroom collapsed under its weight of snow. Possibly this was the part of the new roof the poet Ed had worked on during his shirking period.

Most of Joe's supplies were cut off. Now he needed to devote a part of each day to clearing away the fallen timbers and rubble to get at his food, a task beyond his current strength but not beyond his will.

On a late afternoon, during the tail end of a storm that had been wailing for several days, Joe was astonished to hear a knock on the door. Luckily, the kitchen was situated near the front door or he never would have heard it. Still, he doubted his ears. Maybe it was a tree branch hitting the door from the wind. But he reminded himself there were no trees at this elevation, just boulders, and the wind could not move the boulders, only Kim could.

But the rather light knocking continued.

So he went to the door and opened it. Wonder of wonders, there stood a little boy about five years old. Because the snow came halfway up the door, he stood at eye level with Joe. Joe's first thought was that the spring thaw might have come to the town below so the children had come up the mountain to look for him. But the towering drifts of snow and the large wet intricate flakes still falling belied that notion.

"What miracle is this?" Joe asked in the language of the country. He lifted the boy down to the floor.

"I've come to stay with you," said the boy, in the lilting English of some British Isle. "My name is Jimmy."

"Did you drop from the sky?"

He laughed. "No. I was going to walk all the way, but I got tired so Daddy carried me and Jacob carried Daddy's pack. You see, Jacob came and got us."

Jacob? wondered the holy man.

"Hello, Joe. My name is Errol," said the boy's father, who now appeared at the door. He had bright, intelligent green eyes, black curly hair. The pack on his back, when unmuffled, revealed itself to be a small girl child, lying fast asleep in her cocoon of wraps. "And this is Melissa."

Joe's heart filled with joy to think he would have children here in his mountain fastness, for it truly looked as if this family had come to stay, he knew not why, or how, or from whence.

But it was the boy Joe kept looking at because he felt he knew that dear face, those solemn eyes, the gentle smile.

He was going to close the door and shepherd them to the warm kitchen when a large man appeared through the storm with an enormous pack on his back and it was Jacob, the despondent legionnaire, but his was no longer the sad-eyed face of the grieving warrior—it was ruddy with health and good spirits and the joy of accomplishment. He took off his snowshoes, shook the snow from his coat, then stepped down into the hermitage.

As Joe was about to greet him, he was distracted by

yet another arrival, a slight figure who appeared at the top of the trail and struggled across the yard, buffeted by the wind. She came toward him through the snow, ran the last few steps, and flung herself into his arms. It was Anna. It was the one.

ABOUT THE AUTHOR

Susan Trott is the author of eight previous novels.
She has three grown children, is an ardent
runner, and a homebody who travels widely.
She lives in northern California with a
Norwegian seaman, when he's not at sea.